ROGUE ALPHA

Wild Lake Wolves - Book One

KIMBER WHITE

Nokay Press, LLC

Copyright © 2016 by Kimber White

All rights reserved.

No part of this book may be reproduced in any form or by any electronic or mechanical means, including information storage and retrieval systems, without written permission from the author, except for the use of brief quotations in a book review.

This is a work of fiction. Names, characters, businesses, places, events, and incidents are either the products of the author's imagination or used in a fictitious manner. Any resemblance to actual persons, living or dead, or actual events is purely coincidental.

For all the latest on my new releases and an EXCLUSIVE FREE EBOOK AS A WELCOME GIFT, sign up for my newsletter.
http://www.kimberwhite.com/wild-lake-wolves/wild-lake-wolves-news

Author's Note

The Wild Lake Wolves books have all been written so you can enjoy them as standalones. While they can be read in any order, the events within them do occur chronologically. For a full list of books published books in the series and their recommended reading order, visit the series page at http://www.kimberwhite.com/wild-lake-wolves.

Happy Reading!

Kimber

Chapter One

IT WAS FAINT. Barely more than a blip, but I swear I heard it. I adjusted the pack on my back and pressed the binoculars to my eyes again. Damn. Practically dusk now, it was just too hard to see anything. Maybe if I had night vision goggles. For now though, I just found a clump of leaves and a squirrel darting over a fallen log just ahead of me. A breeze picked up from the north, rustling its way through the canopy of elm and birch trees surrounding me.

Blip.

There it was again. I shut my eyes and pressed the headset to my ears. I turned up the volume and waited.

Nothing.

"Come on, Bambi," I whispered. "Give Mama a sign."

Still nothing.

I checked my watch. Six forty-five. I was supposed to be back at the outpost by seven. I'd never make that, but if I got lucky and found our little wayward fawn, I didn't figure anyone would get angry with me about it.

An arcing call pierced through the stillness, followed by another. Shit. Turkey buzzards. I saw three of the fat bastards circling overhead. Not a good sign. One of them swooped down and disappeared below the trees just a few yards in front of me. Dread filled me as I made my way toward it. Again, I turned up the volume on my headset hoping against hope I'd hear that little blip indicating our guy was still on the move.

"Prince!" The voice vibrated at my hip. Squatting as I was, it startled me enough to make me lose my balance, and I fell on my ass in a wet pile of rotting leaves. I turned the volume down on the walkie as I pulled it out of my hip holster.

"Where are you?"

I brought the walkie to my mouth. No point in whispering now. Any wildlife around me would have run for cover after that lack of grace.

"Just past the 14 trail marker. I thought I had Number 11 tracked. I'm pretty sure his signal just cut out. Hoping it's faulty wiring. I just want to check it out and I'm heading right back."

My professor grumbled through the speaker and my heart dropped a little. It sounded like I'd set off his legendary short fuse. Most of the students in my program didn't like to work with him because of it. But, so far I'd been spared. He'd treated me like gold. The Teacher's Pet nickname stuck with me, but I didn't care. It was all in their heads. And I was here to learn. Professor Flood only picked one student each year to work on this grant. Experience like this could help me land a spot in the biology graduate program down the road.

"That's too far to go on your own." Professor Flood's voice sounded measured, but not angry. Yet. "It's getting dark. I'll come to you. I'm about four hundred meters out to the east of you. Stay put."

Four hundred meters? What the hell were four hundred meters? Give it to me in feet, miles.

"I really think he's right head of me. Carrion-eaters just above me. Let me just make sure."

"Laura. For once will you just do what you're told?"

Yikes. Here came the Floodgates, as everyone called them. I guess it was finally my turn to be the target of them. But, by the time I waited for him to get out here, there wouldn't be much left of whatever carcass those birds zoned in on. If I found our little guy with the tracking tag, Flood couldn't stay mad at me. It would save the program a couple thousand dollars.

I pushed back the brush. In a small clearing at the foot of a birch tree, I found what the birds did. My heart dropped. God, I hoped it wasn't him.

"Shoo!" I made as much noise as I could, tromping through the sticks and brambles. The birds cawed at me. Three of them surrounded the red-spotted clump of fur near the tree. One of them raised its wings, protecting his soon-to-be dinner behind him. Up close, these beasties were massive, their heads coming up almost to my knee.

"Shoo!" I waved my arms and pushed past them, hoping they'd fly away. But, I was most definitely on their turf tonight. They hopped into the brush but stayed close. Sighing, I dropped down to my knees.

Number 11.

He'd laid down in the soft pile of leaves, his gangly legs drawn up beneath him. Only about the size of a Cocker Spaniel, he had a row of white spots in a perfect line down his back. Three white spots clumped together near his rump, two on top, one at the center. It looked like a Mickey Mouse silhouette. I pulled a pair of purple latex gloves out of my pack and checked the small, green tag on his left ear just to be sure. He had a GPS microchip tracker embedded just beneath the skin on his shoulder that transmitted his location on software back at the lab.

"Poor baby," I whispered, smoothing his ears back. He was still warm, his body stiffening. But, his sightless eyes had pearled over as he stared into the woods before him. The birds hadn't gotten to him yet. I couldn't find any visible signs of injury on him. But, with his mother nowhere to be found, the little guy was never going to last too long out here. Her beacon had stopped transmitting almost two days ago.

I took the pliers out of my pack and popped the tag off his ear. We'd learn crucial information about Number 11's last days back at the lab. I bagged the tag and sealed it carefully into the outer compartment of my pack.

"Sorry buddy," I said. "Wish I could do more for you, but circle of life and all."

One of the turkey vultures cawed at me.

"Yeah. Well, you don't have to brag about it, asshole. Wait your turn. I'm almost done."

I took the digital camera from my pocket and snapped a few pictures of Number 11 for Professor Flood's white board. Then, I zipped the camera in my pack and pulled the gloves off my hands. I was running out of places to stow stuff so I pulled the pack off my shoulder and squatted down to find a plastic refuse bag. They must have smashed their way down to the bottom of my pack past water bottles, notepads, and a bunch of other things I probably could have left back at the cabin.

The turkey vultures clacked behind me then screeched so loudly I covered my ears. "God, could you at least wait until I'm gone!"

But the vultures took flight in unison, and their loud shouts of protest echoed through the forest.

"What the hell made you give up so easily?"

I froze. The hairs on the back of my neck stood on end. Something big had chased the birds away. That same something was behind me. On some preternatural level, I could feel it watching me through the trees. All other sounds in the forest went dead quiet. My own pulse beat loudly between my ears.

I turned. Slowly.

Two blazing eyes hovered between the trees about five yards straight ahead of me. My heart hammered in my chest as I carefully rose to my feet. I clutched the pack to my chest, thinking maybe I could hurl it at whatever lurked in front of me. That ought to be enough to scare it off.

Then the creature stepped out of the shadows and I dropped the pack to my feet.

A black wolf with piercing gold eyes took two slow steps toward me. His massive paws made barely a sound as he moved through the blanket of leaves. His ears pricked and he chuffed once, pawing the ground. He kept his eyes locked with mine displaying a keen intelligence that both hypnotized me and made my heart race even faster. Should I run? Should I make myself look bigger? We didn't cover wolves during training, for God's sake! This was western Michigan. They didn't hunt this far south.

I moved toward him. I don't know why I did it. Some rational part of my brain told me to scream, to run, to find the biggest stick I could and throw it at him. But, the wolf kept coming toward me. Something seemed familiar about him, absurd as I knew that was. He bared his teeth and let out a low, vibrating sound that seemed to penetrate my skin and warm my blood.

I put a hand out. Something made me want to touch him though my fingers trembled before me. The wolf pawed the ground again but didn't move away. His golden eyes flashed, changing, narrowing, becoming almost human for an instant. But, that couldn't be. None of this could. This felt like a waking dream. Not real. Too incredible.

I stepped forward, reaching out. The wolf was just a few inches from me. The world was the sound of my own breath hitching as I finally threaded my fingers through his coarse, dark fur, placing each hand just below his ears, tilting his head toward me.

And more incredible still, he let me. He let out a few quick pants, and cocked his head, but he didn't shy away. That low vibration in his throat seemed to fill me as if I were making the sound with him.

"Who are you?" I don't know whether I voiced those words aloud or just thought them. The wolf blinked slowly once, twice, but he didn't shy away as I kept my hands on his head. He seemed to be asking me the very same question.

I leaned down, bring my face level with his. The fur on the back of his neck stood on end and he pricked his ears but still, he didn't stop me. His breath blew hot against my skin and he searched my face with those fiery golden eyes. We stood like that for a few moments, transfixed by each other. I felt his power between my fingertips as I ran my hand down from the dome of his head, across his back. He had thick, corded muscles through his shoulders that rippled as he shifted his weight from one front paw and the other. He seemed to be deciding whether to stay put or run himself.

"It's okay." This time I did speak out loud. "What are you doing all the way down here? Are you lost?"

Some rational part of my brain told me I should try and tag him too. Or at least get a picture. No one would ever believe me that I'd found him this far south. I couldn't though. I could barely move. At least, not until the next instant when everything changed.

Thunder cracked all around me. The wolf's eyes widened and he jerked backward, breaking the link between us. The wolf let out a growl that ricocheted off the trees and stirred my own blood. He was hit. Wounded. It all happened in an instant but red blossomed above his left eye. His blood sprayed across my hands. But, he moved so fast I saw only a streak of black as he disappeared into the trees again.

"Get down!"

I came back into myself. Professor Flood stood in the clearing bracing his shotgun against his shoulder. Shaking, I dropped to my knees, my hands on fire where the wolf's blood coated my palms.

Chapter Two

"JESUS. LAURA. ARE YOU ALL RIGHT?"

My ears still rang from the shotgun blast. Professor Flood brought the gun down and came to me. He put a hand on my shoulder and shook me gently.

"Laura. Are you all right?"

I shook my head. "You shot him?"

I held my hands in front of me. Professor Flood put the shotgun down and grabbed my wrists. He drew me to my feet.

"It's not my blood," I said. "I'm okay. You didn't have to do that."

He pulled a white handkerchief out of his pocket and wrapped it around my hands, wiping off most of the blood. I jerked my hands away. I didn't want him to touch me, to touch any part of the wolf, strange as that seemed. Shock. I must be in shock.

"Why did you do that? That wasn't a dart. That was a 12 gauge! Jesus, you could have taken my head off."

"Not even close," he said. "And I didn't shoot at him. I shot high. But you can't be too careful. I warned you the coyotes out here are extremely aggressive. That's why you're not supposed to venture off this far alone, Laura. Especially with it getting so dark. That could have been much, much worse. We've got black bears out here too."

"What?"

Professor Flood grabbed my backpack and held out his hand to help me up. I shook it off and rose to my feet. "I'm okay."

"That wasn't a coyote. You saw it. You shot at it. What are you talking about?"

Professor Flood froze and turned toward me. He ran a hand through his light brown hair. He had a cowlick at the front that never laid flat. It lent a boyishness to his looks along with his perpetually tanned skin and piercing blue eyes. Eyes that stared at me now as if I were speaking Martian.

"Yes. I know exactly what I saw. Why the hell didn't you stay where I told you to?"

"What?" My mind raced. My heart still beat in my throat. I struggled to grasp something normal. Something to get my pulse to beat steady again. I looked down at my discarded pack, the patch of leaves on the ground. "Oh. Number 11."

My hands still shaking, I pointed back at the birch tree where the little fawn had fallen. Flood stepped around me and went to it.

He shook his head. "Damn. I was hoping that little guy would make it. No sign of injury?"

"No. He looks like he just went to sleep like that."

"Hmm. Well, while we're out here. Might as well make some use of it. You think you've got a hold of yourself?"

I bit my lip past the comment I wanted to make. *You mean since you shot at my fucking head?* "I'm fine."

"Good. You have any specimen containers in your pack? I've got a flashlight. Why don't we see if we can find any droppings nearby?"

Droppings.

I smacked my palm against the side of my head, trying literally to knock myself back to the present. Droppings. Right. I pulled a fresh pair of gloves out of my pack and a specimen container.

"It's not glamorous," Flood said as he shone the light in a circle around where Number 11 rested. "But I don't have the equipment or funding for autopsies or blood samples. Poop. We can do poop."

"Right."

"Bingo!" Flood stopped a few feet from the fawn and shook the light. "Bag it up."

I raised a brow at him but went to the spot on the ground he indicated. Then I bagged the poop.

"Congratulations, Miss Prince. You're on your way to becoming a bona fide biologist now."

I sealed the container and disposed of my gloves with the other. I held the container out to Professor Flood, but he just smiled. "That's all you."

"Right. Lucky me."

"Come on. If we hurry back, there might be some pizza left for you."

"You ordered without me?"

Flood shrugged and smoothed his cowlick back. It fell right back in front of his face a second later. He shot me a dazzling smile and put a hand on the small of my back, making my skin prickle just a little. "I told you to be back by six thirty. You try making Cameron and the others wait when there's food involved. Don't know where that kid puts it. He's got a hollow leg or something."

Cameron Davies was Professor Flood's favorite graduate assistant. He, Professor Flood, and I made up the team from Great Lakes University until the end of the summer semester. Another group of researchers from Michigan State shared the camp with us. We had help from the D.N.R. and the Manistee Park Ranger Service, but this was all Flood's show. Tracking Chronic Wasting Disease or C.W.D. in a particular herd of white-tailed deer that had been given certain antibiotics within the first few months of their lives. So far, the results had been dismal. The animals were still getting sick. Still dying.

Flood had parked the Jeep at the entrance to the trail. I hopped in the passenger side and put my pack in the seat behind me. As Flood started up the vehicle, I turned to him.

"That wasn't a coyote back there," I said. "Didn't you see it? It was a wolf. A great big wolf."

Flood smiled when he looked at me. I'd seen him flash that smirk in class. It was kind of his trademark. It's why most of the girls sat in the front row, for a chance of having it directed straight at them. Then they'd leave class giggling and whispering to each other about Byron Flood and his killer dimples. For me though? Right now? It felt patronizing.

Rogue Alpha

"You've been out here too long," he said. "Don't worry. Tomorrow's going to be a down day. I was hoping you'd come into town with me. We need to stock up on some supplies. I'm making my famous chili tomorrow night. One of the perks of being my summer assistant, I let you in on the secret formula."

He wagged his eyebrows up and down. I rolled my eyes at him and crossed my arms in front of me. Then I shifted in my seat to stare straight ahead. We rode in silence the rest of the way. We made the steep turn up to the Great Lakes University Center for Wildlife Conservation. A fancy name for a row of five rustic log cabins. Only two had electricity by way of a portable generator and running water. One, we used as a mess hall and meeting area. The other was our lab. As the only woman in the group this summer, I got the luxury of being the only one out here besides Flood with a cabin to myself. Cameron shared his cabin with six students from M.S.U. out here working a different C.W.D. based grant. They kept to themselves except for chow time.

As Flood pulled up alongside the mess hall, Cameron came out licking the thumb of one hand while folding a giant slice of Chicago-style pizza in the other. He made a great show out of cocking his head back and taking a bite. He shot me a wink as I climbed out of the car.

"Any of that left or did you mongrels eat it all?" I slugged Cam in the shoulder.

Cam gave me a sly grin. He had the warmest brown eyes and thick black hair that parted down the middle. A birthmark on his scalp resulted in a thick, white stripe of hair along the left side. The scar from his harelip gave him a permanent lopsided grin that actually fit his personality pretty well.

"There's half a pie left of the sausage and anchovies."

"Gross." I wrinkled my nose. "You guys suck."

"I told her." Flood stepped around us. He had my bag slung over his shoulder along with his own. He tossed mine to me. I got my hands up just in time to catch it. "Hurry up and grab a slice. You can pick off what you don't like. Then, have Cam take you to the lab and show you how to set up the slides for that specimen."

Then Flood turned and took the steps into the mess hall three at a time with an athletic stride.

"I'll wait for you," Cam said.

I shook my head. "No thanks. Between the anchovies and the poop samples in my bag, my appetite is pretty much gone."

Cam put an arm around me. "You'll get used to it. Poop is life. Come on. Plus, I lied. I hid a couple of slices of pepperoni in the back of the fridge for you."

I leaned up and kissed Cameron on the cheek. "You're all right, you know that? No matter what those assholes from State say about you when you're not listening."

Cam reared back, his mouth went wide. "What do you mean? What do they say about me?"

I reached up, tussled his hair, and started walking to the cabin lab. Cameron Davies had genius-level intelligence, but he worried way too much about what other people thought of him. And, he was gullible. I gave him a raised eyebrow over my shoulder to let him know I was only kidding. He flipped me off and followed me into the lab.

"Watch it," he said. "I'm about to teach you how not to get deer shit all over yourself. You wouldn't want me to forget a step."

"If I can't figure that out myself, I have bigger problems."

I popped the screen door and stepped into the cabin, fumbling with the switch against the wall. The overhead fluorescents blinked to life, casting the whole room in flickering yellow. It took a few minutes for the generator to power the things all the way. The lab consisted of four long, white folding tables with various specimen jars covering them along with two large microscopes. We had three industrial-sized refrigerators in one corner and our computers in the other and storage lockers in the other. The walls were covered with maps of the area and Professor Flood's whiteboards. I was still trying to get the hang of how to decipher his scrawling handwriting and shorthand.

"Take the stuff to the second table," Cam said. I opened my pack and pulled out the specimen jar while Cam fired up the microscope, readied a few slides, and pulled a wheeled stool up to the table. He kicked the second stool toward me. I stopped it with my knee and scooted over to join him.

As I set the container on the table, my hands still shook. Cam shot me a quizzical look and waited while I tried to unscrew the cap.

"Put some gloves on first," Cam said, tossing a fresh pair of purple ones at me.

"Right."

"First rule of not getting shit all over you."

"Right. Right. I got it." I handed the jar to Cam.

"You okay? You're shaking like a leaf. Did something happen out there?"

Cam's expression darkened. He pursed his lips together and peered at me over his thick glasses.

"What? No. I'm okay." For the briefest moment, I hesitated before telling Cam about the wolf. Professor Flood had acted strangely. Maybe Cam would too. But, Cam and I had been working together for two semesters now. He knew me well enough to know when I was bullshitting him. Still, an odd feeling speared through me when I thought of that dark wolf and his golden eyes. My heart fluttered and I felt . . . protective of it somehow. As if telling anyone else about that brief moment between us would betray the wolf in some way. Silly. I shook my head as if I could physically drive away those thoughts.

"Laura?"

Cam reached into the container and took the sample out using tweezers. He placed a small amount between the slides and gave the rest of it back to me.

"Well. It's kind of hard to explain. But, uh, I ran into a wolf out there. A big-ass black one."

Cameron dropped the tweezers and sat back. "You did what now?"

I bit my lip. "Yeah. A wolf. Came right up to me. I think it was just as interested in the fawn as I was."

Cam whistled low. "This far south? There are known packs in the Upper Peninsula. Not down here. You sure it wasn't a . . ."

I put my hand up. "It wasn't a coyote, Cam. I know the fucking difference."

Cam cocked his head to the side. "Easy. I'm just asking the question. Jeez."

"I'm sorry. Ugh. It got really close. I mean. I, uh, I sort of got to pet it."

"You pet it? You pet a wolf."

I shrugged, realizing now how ridiculous the story sounded as soon as I said it out loud. Well, no going back now. "Kind of. Then Flood showed up. Cam, he shot at it. Not darts. With the 12 gauge."

A muscle twitched near Cameron's left eye. He let out a sharp exhale. "Are you fucking serious?"

I nodded. "Shot ricocheted off the trees or something. Grazed it." I looked down. I hadn't noticed before, but a few drops of drying blood clung to the sleeve of my gray hoodie. I held my hand out and showed Cam.

"He got away. The wolf did. Ran off quick as a bolt of lightning after that."

"Wouldn't you?"

I got up and looked out the front door. For some reason, I thought it best if no one overheard this conversation. Again, that strange protectiveness rose up in me.

"Why the fuck did he shoot at it?"

Turning, I went back to my stool and pulled it up even closer to Cam so he could hear me when I whispered. "That's the thing. I have no clue. What was he doing with live ammo in the first place? Seriously. He dinged the wolf, but he could just as easily have got me. He was about a hundred yards away. And Cam. He insisted it was a coyote. I swear to you. It wasn't. It was a big, black wolf with fiery eyes. How in the hell could he mistake one for the other? I've never seen a black coyote, have you?"

Cam smiled. "Never seen a black wolf either, Laura. Not in western Michigan. Look, if you say it was a wolf, it was a wolf. You sure there isn't the slightest slim chance Flood was right?"

My blood boiled. Cam saw the anger cross my face. He put his hands up in surrender and scooted his chair back. "All right. All right. Black wolf. No question. Got it."

I curled my hand into a fist, shook at him and tapped his nose. "Good. Don't make me have to bust you up."

Cam smiled and gestured to the poop specimen I'd left sitting on the table. "You get the fun job. Sift through that bad boy and see if you can find anything interesting Bambi might have eaten."

"Gross."

"Remember," Cam started. I sighed and raised a brow at him. Then I finished his sentence with him.

"Poop is life."

Chapter Three

THE WOLF SURROUNDED ME. His hot breath skittered across the back of my neck. His golden eyes hovered above me, just out of reach. My feet tangled in the bedsheets, holding me back when he turned and beckoned me to follow. I reached forward, wanting to touch him again. My heart pounded. His thick fur, both coarse and silky, tickled my fingertips. But, he was just out of reach.

My spine turned liquid as his howl rose in the darkness. It filled me from the inside out, raising the hair on the back of my neck, washing over me with heat and power. I wanted to run beside him. I wanted to bury my face in the downy fur of his neck, feel the coiled power of the muscles that formed his haunches just before he leaped away from me into the darkness.

Then, the world exploded in sound and light.

"Laura!"

Down was up. I clawed at the ground. I must have tried to get out of bed, but tangled in the sheets, I landed on the ground.

Professor Flood pounded on the screen door once, then came inside. Panic filled my heart as I tried to get free of the sheets. I wore nothing but a black lace bra and matching panties. A thin sheen of sweat coated my skin as I struggled to cover myself before Flood stepped around the bed.

"Wait!" I finally got my leg out of the sheet and tried to pull it up to cover me.

But Flood stood at the foot of the bed. He turned his back to me, but not before I saw his eyes blaze with naked lust as he raked them over me.

"Can you wait outside?" I shouted.

"Uh. I'm sorry. Jesus. I'm really sorry. You were shouting. I thought you were hurt."

"What? No. I'm fine. I was sleeping."

"Hmm." Flood straightened his shoulders. He didn't turn back around as I pulled the sheets around me and stood up. But, he didn't leave the room either. "Well, you sleep loud then, I guess."

"Please, just wait outside. What time is it?"

"What? Oh. It's just after nine. You're late. You were supposed to meet me down at the mess hall. You're coming with me into town remember?"

Shit. Right. Why the hell hadn't my alarm gone off? I reached for my phone. The damn thing had dislodged from the charging dock. It was dead.

"Can you give me fifteen minutes?" I said, feeling a little embarrassed. On the other hand, Flood still hadn't done the decent thing and gotten the hell out of my room.

"Sure," he said. He finally started walking toward the door. "But hurry up. It's Sunday. The Fleegers close the store up by eleven thirty so they can make the noon mass on time. It's a thirty-minute drive. We needed to be on the road twenty minutes ago."

"I'll just be a second," I yelled as Professor Flood stepped out of my cabin and let the door close behind him.

"Shit. Shit. Shit!" I had just one pair of clean jeans and a t-shirt left. We went to the laundromat in town on Monday nights. I pulled on my clothes as fast as I could, wrapped my hair in a topknot and grabbed a toothbrush. I didn't know whether to be angrier with myself for oversleeping, or with Flood for invading my personal space in a huge way. For the moment, I'd settle for just getting the hell down to the mess hall and salvaging what I could of the morning.

As I stepped out into the sunlight, a shiver ran through me, strong enough to take my breath away for an instant. I turned, but not fast enough. A streak of black moved in my peripheral vision. But, there was nothing there. Just rustling tree branches, waving in the breeze.

I pressed my thumbs against my eyes to clear away the cobwebs clouding my thoughts. Flood had torn me out of a deep sleep and some intense dream. Still, I couldn't shake the feeling that someone or something watched me through that tree line.

"Boo!"

I jumped.

"Son of a bitch!"

Cam jumped out from behind my cabin. He held a piece of cold pizza in his hand on a napkin.

"Why didn't you come get me?" I asked. "Flood's on a war path. My damn phone died in the middle of the night. It never went off."

Cam shrugged. "Sorry. I got up early and did some work in the lab. But, here's a peace offering. He won't wait for you to get breakfast. Better get your ass moving."

I took the pizza from Cam just as Flood laid on the Jeep's horn. It was time to go.

"Don't forget popcorn," Cam called out as I bounded down the cabin steps and headed for the Jeep. "The kind we make over the campfire!"

I raised two fingers above my head and waved at Cam. Then, I hopped into the Jeep, shoving pizza down my head as quickly as I could.

A good ten minutes went by before either of us said anything. I couldn't tell if Flood was angry for having been delayed or still feeling a little awkward for staring at me in my underwear. I couldn't decide if I was angrier at him for that or awkward for being late. Finally, Flood spoke first.

"Yeah. Um. I'm sorry about that back there. I really did think something happened to you. You were, um, screaming, Laura. Like you were hurt. You sure you're okay?"

Color warmed my cheeks. "Oh. It's okay." A part of me wanted to kick myself for letting him off the hook. Except, I'd been dreaming about the wolf when he burst in. I didn't remember screaming, but I remembered the whole thing was pretty intense. Maybe I *did* scream.

"I'm kind of used to not getting a lot of privacy back home," I said. "Big family. Five brothers. Three sisters."

Flood let out a whistle. "Wow. I mean, seriously. Wow. Nine children? I didn't think people did that anymore."

I nodded. "Old school Catholic parents."

"Where are you in all of that?"

"Smack in the middle. I've got a pair of brothers and sisters above me, a pair below."

"Ah. Well, that explains why you were so eager to hightail it out of there this summer."

I laughed. He wasn't wrong. I loved my family, but the decision to live on campus at G.L.U. had been one of the best I'd ever made. It was the first time I'd ever had a bathroom to myself. To me, dorm life actually brought peace and quiet. When the opportunity to join Flood's team this summer came along, it seemed like heaven. Until the last twenty-four hours, it pretty much had been. Now though, something filled me with unease.

I pressed my forehead against the window as the trees flew by. We were deep in the Huron-Manistee National Forest miles away from anything resembling civilization, and I kind of loved it.

"Where's home?"

"Green Bluff, California."

"Well, that's a long way from home. How'd you end up at Great Lakes U?" Flood asked.

I shrugged. "Ah. That's an easy one. They offered me a full ride. I did well on my S.A.Ts. G.L.U. was the farthest from home willing to pay for me. So, here I am."

"Good choice. When's the last time you went back?"

I shrugged. "Not since Christmas." It wasn't that I didn't miss my family. I did. But being away gave me freedom from the chaos large families bring. I loved my time on my own.

"Well, I for one am damn glad you decided to give us a try. You're talented, Laura. Gifted even. You have a drive and aptitude I don't often see in girls your age."

I bristled a little at the word "girl," but decided to let it slide this time. He was trying to give me a compliment, and I appreciated it.

"I mean it. You could go very far in this field if that's what you're truly interested in. You know the biology graduate program at G.L.U. is very competitive. Very competitive. We only let in a handful of students each year. How long before you get your bachelor's?"

I bit my lip. This early in the semester, I hadn't even dreamed of approaching Professor Flood for a recommendation. Most graduate program students went on to their dream jobs after finishing. "Uh. I need about fifty more credits. So, a year and a half if I push it."

Flood smiled as he pulled into the parking lot of Fleeger's General Store. "Well, push it, Laura. You know, we've got a full day planned, but I'd like to talk to you about this a little later. How about at dinner?"

My mouth went dry. Flood reached over and rested his arm across my seat back. He dipped his head and flashed me the smile that made the front row girls swoon. It made me uncomfortable on every level. He reached up with his other hand and brushed a hair out of my eyes. His was close enough for me to feel his breath against my ear.

"We should get in there," I said. "It's almost ten thirty. You said the Fleegers need to close up for mass. Are you ready, Professor Flood?"

He picked a piece of lint off my shoulder. "It's Byron. When we're out here. Just Byron. When we're on campus, different story. But, we've got a lot of weeks out here in the wilderness to be so formal."

"Sure." I reached for the door and stumbled a little getting out of the car. Flood's soft laughter followed me as I walked up the wooden stairs into the store. My pulse quickened as I reached for the door. My palms sweated and the air around me seemed to thicken. I reached for the door with shaky fingers. Flood's shadow fell over me as he followed me up the stairs. I didn't want him to touch me again. The implications of his tone of voice, his gestures, were unmistakable.

"Wait up, Laura," he said, his rich tenor prickling along my spine. "Let me at least be a gentleman and get the door for you."

His put his hand on my back and reached around me for the door handle. Before he could open it though, the door flew inward. Flood's fingers flexed where he held them to my back and I looked up to face a mountain.

"She looks capable of handling doorknobs all by herself." The mountain had a voice. A deep, rich, baritone. My eyes started at his chest. He wore a black t-shirt stretched taut over hard muscles. I followed those muscles up until I met his eyes as they flashed gold fire. Hair black as midnight long enough to just graze his shoulders. High, strong cheekbones over rough, dark stubble. Perfect, pale, full lips set into a hard line as he stared down Byron Flood over my shoulder. He filled the doorway with his broad shoulders, muscled thighs thick as tree trunks wrapped in denim. Worn, black motorcycle boots that looked solid enough to kick through a wall.

He had a fresh cut above his left eye. It made a jagged line like a lightning bolt through the dark, thatch of his brow. Instinct or insanity made me reach up and hover my finger over the wound. He flinched, drew back. My fingers froze in midair for just a moment before I dropped my hand to my side.

"That's a nasty cut," I said. "You should ice that."

He gave me a half smile that sent heat zinging through me. Shit. I was acting just like one of Flood's front row girls. One muscle-bound biker type gives me a wink and I go all gushy inside.

"Thanks for the tip," he said. His eyes went back to Flood and he took a step back to let me in through the door. When Flood tried to follow, he puffed his chest out and a did a little man-spreading that made Flood brush against his shoulder as he passed.

"You hassling my customers Mr. Devane?" A high pitched male voice came from the back of the store.

Mr. Devane. It didn't suit him. He should be Mr. Tank. Mr. Rock. Devane sounded civilized. Refined. This man seemed wild and raw like he belonged to the woods around us.

"You tell me. You feeling hassled?" Devane looked at me, his eyes seared straight through me then he flicked them to Flood behind me, his implication clear.

"I'm good," I answered. It was true and not true. But, as I stood just a few feet from this man, I had a sense that every question, every gesture he made was part of some kind of threat assessment. He stood with his body angled toward the door, his legs slightly parted as if he were ready for a fight. His eyes scanned the room from me to Flood then back to the door.

But, whoever he was, I needed him to know I could handle myself. I don't know why that was so important, but it was. "Are you feeling hassled Professor Flood?" I emphasized the word Professor. The man was in serious need of a reminder of boundaries. Might as well start there.

His mouth set into a grim line, and his face had drained of color. "Let's just get what we need and get out of here. You've set us behind schedule enough."

I've what now? Flood was seething rage. He brushed fully past Devane and grabbed a basket from the wall, gripping it so hard he bent the handle. He moved to the other end of the store and away from Devane and me.

"Didn't mean to upset him," Devane said. "Seems a little touchy."

"We're here for research," I said stupidly.

Devane raised his uninjured eyebrow. I looked in front of me. I happened to be standing in front of the first aid supplies and over-the-counter medicine. I grabbed a bottle of iodine and gauze and thrust it into Devane's hand. My skin flared hot where he touched me, sending a sensation like a shock wave through me.

"I think you might have a fever, Mr. Devane," I said, my mouth going instantly dry.

"I'm not Mr. Devane. I'm Mal."

Mal. His name washed over me in ripples. Mal. It suited him. Bad. Dangerous.

"Well, it's nice to meet you, Mal. But that eye of yours might be infected." I grabbed a tube of triple antibiotic cream and shoved that in his hand next.

His posture changed. His shoulders dropped and he shook with low, rumbling laughter. He took the tube from me and held it up, shaking it once. "I'll take that into consideration."

"How'd you get that cut? It looks bad." And it did. A chunk of skin had been torn away just above his eyebrow. When it healed, the hair likely wouldn't grow back, so he'd have a permanent line running through his brow to make him look even more dangerous than he already did.

His face grew serious again. He looked over my shoulder. I looked back. Flood stood at the checkout counter, his basket heaping with supplies as he fumbled for his wallet to pay Mr. Fleeger.

"Hunting accident," Mal said, not taking his eyes off Flood.

"Hmm. You'd better be more careful next time. Wear more orange."

"Thanks for the tip," Mal said, his voice smooth and deep.

"Do you know him?" I asked, lowering my voice. He kept his gaze locked on Flood, watching every move he took through the store.

Mal's eyes finally flicked back to me. They were deep set, a golden amber color like scotch whiskey with gold flecks. Beautiful eyes. Mesmerizing. But familiar. Recognition skittered across my skin, making the tiny hairs on my arms stand on end.

"Research," Mal said the word as if it tasted bad in his mouth. "What's he researching?"

I shook the cobwebs from my head. "Chronic Wasting Disease in the whitetail population around here."

"Hmm." He shrugged his shoulders and jerked his chin, almost scoffing at my answer.

I meant to ask him what he meant by that but didn't get the chance. Flood pushed his way down the aisle, his arms laden with three stuffed grocery bags. I turned and took one from him.

"We need to go," he said, physically putting himself between me and Mal Devane. It seemed a risky maneuver. Mal looked like he could squash him with one fist. Flood was by no means slight. He too was strong, with sculpted muscles. But his were just that, sculpted. He'd earned them on weight machines in a gym somewhere. Mal looked like he'd earned his splitting logs or moving boulders.

Then Flood moved past me and out the door, leaving me literally holding the bag and alone with Mal Devane.

"You need to watch out for him," Mal said and it startled me. I didn't know this guy. He seemed familiar, sure, but it meant nothing.

"I know," I heard myself saying. It was the truth, after all. I looked back up at him.

Mal reached over me and held the door open. I ducked under his massive arm and went out on the porch.

"Take care of that cut," I said, turning back to him. "It was nice to meet you."

Mal said nothing. He just focused that laser stare on me. What happened next, I couldn't be sure I remembered right later. It was just a fraction of a second. An instant. But those amber eyes flashed gold, sending a shock of fire through me.

I didn't know what it meant. Who he was. But I couldn't shake the feeling that I had seen him somewhere before. Or the knowledge that I'd see him again. Soon.

Chapter Four

WHEN WE GOT BACK to the outpost, Flood wouldn't talk to me. He slammed the car door shut and stormed off to the lab, leaving me alone to unpack the groceries. Never mind the lack of chivalry, I was kind of glad to have him out of my hair. I gathered as much as I could and hauled it back to the mess hall cabin.

After I got that sorted, I headed back to the Jeep for the second load. Before I got there, I saw Flood standing a few yards away from the vehicle talking to a man I'd never seen before. This guy was big, broad, and kind of built like Devane, the man I'd met at the general store. But, in contrast to Devane's dark hair, this guy was a ginger. He towered over Flood and kept his fists curled at his sides, and in a ready stance like he could snap at any moment.

I don't know what made me do it, but I ducked behind the nearest cabin and listened.

"Our deal is for you and your boys. I can't have you bringing any more outsiders into the park."

Flood's companion gripped Flood's shoulder hard enough that I saw him wince. "You don't need to worry about the terms of our deal. They are whatever I say they are."

"Hey, you need *me*, remember? You want the rangers to leave you alone, you go through me."

The bigger man's eyes flashed hot, again, reminding me a little of Mal Devane's. The air around me seemed charged as if I were about to witness something I shouldn't.

"You'll deal with the rangers or you'll deal with the whole pack of us. You keep thinking you've got some kind of bargaining power over me. You think I couldn't rip my way through this camp and destroy it in about five minutes if I wanted to? You're a convenience, Flood. That's all. Now, tell me again who you think you saw out there."

Flood sighed and ran a hand through his hair, attempting to flatten his cowlick again. "The black one. The one you said you were looking for. Big fucker."

I stopped breathing, straining to hear every word. The black one. He was talking about the wolf. The wolf he denied even existed. What else could he have meant?

The man drew his head back and I saw a muscle jump in his jaw. His eyes narrowed, filling with menace. "You see him again, you call me right away. Why the fuck am I hearing about this the day after?"

Flood opened and closed his mouth like a fish, searching for an answer. "Next time I will. Didn't realize it was that urgent to you."

"It's not your job to worry about what's important and what isn't. It's your job to tell me what you see. That's all. Are we clear?"

Flood nodded. "Yeah. Got it."

"Good. Every time I have to come down here, it's a risk to me and my people. Don't give me a reason to have to do it again."

"I-I know. And I told you. I handled it anyway. But, you gotta promise me he won't come back here or bring any others. I've got a group of people around here that are trained to look for stuff like that. I don't have control over the people from the other school. If word gets out, they'll bring dozens more. That's not good for either of us."

"You let me worry about that. You just keep up your end."

"I am. I will. Nobody's going to mess with you around here."

"Good. Then we're clear."

Flood nodded like a bobble head and the guy finally took his strong hand off his shoulder. He tore off toward the woods with speed that made him a blur. I blinked my eyes. He moved so fast it didn't seem human before he disappeared beyond the tree line, leaving Flood standing there awkwardly.

Again, I don't know what compelled me to do it, but I moved further back behind the cabin, not wanting to be seen. The groceries could wait. Finally, Flood left and disappeared into his own cabin.

I didn't see him again until a few hours later, but Flood was on edge the rest of the day. He barely spoke to me except to bark orders. He sent Cameron and me on a hike to collect more samples. We went deeper into the woods than the day before but found basically nothing. We had four more fawns with tracking devices but got no signal from any of them today. It was a bad sign. It meant they weren't moving.

"What the hell happened between you two today?" Cam

finally asked after Flood got short with me over the walkie for about the sixth time in an hour.

"What do you mean?"

"I mean why's he riding you so hard today? He usually saves that shit for me."

I squatted in front of a tree, brushing away a group of matted leaves looking for trail markings. I smoothed a hair out of my face and shielded my eyes from the sun. Cam stood a few feet away from me. I chewed my bottom lip debating whether to tell Cam about the red-headed stranger I saw talking to Flood and how it unsettled him. I decided against it for now, but there was still something gnawing at me.

"Do I need to worry about him?" I asked. "I mean really worry about him?"

Cam turned the knob on his walkie to off and shoved it in the holster he had hooked to his belt. "Meaning?"

"Meaning, does that asshole have a reputation with female interns I need to know about?"

Cam let out a heavy sigh that pretty much answered my burning questions.

"Great," I said, brushing off my knees, I stood. "Are you serious? Is that the deal with him? Is that why I'm here?"

Cam put his hands out in a defensive posture. "Whoa. Just whoa. I never said that. I don't know that. Honest."

"But you know something or you wouldn't be acting like that. Come on, Cam. I need you to be my friend, not my T.A."

"What's he said to you?"

My turn to let out a heavy sigh. "Nothing. Nothing overt

anyway. It's just a vibe. Some boundary issues." I hesitated to tell him about Flood coming into my room this morning while I was in my bra and underwear. I should have. I know this. But, a part of me wanted to believe Flood's explanation. I *had* had an intense dream or nightmare. He *might* have heard me screaming. But, his creepy behavior in the car wasn't something I misinterpreted. At all.

"He said he wanted to talk to me over dinner about my prospects in the graduate program."

Cam's eyes widened. "And you think that's a bad thing? Shit. Laura. That's exciting. You know how competitive the program is? Even I didn't get in on my first try. And I know you know how brilliant I am."

"Shut it. I'm serious. I need to know what I'm getting myself into with him. You've worked with him for two years. Give me something. I can handle it if I know what I'm walking into."

Cam shrugged. He wouldn't meet my eyes, and that had big, fat alarm bells ringing in my head.

"Great." I punched my fist into my thigh and tried to brush past him on the trail. Cam put a hand on my shoulder to stop me.

"Laura. Just hang on. Look, I'm not going to deny the guy's vain. He doesn't hate the fact that the girls in his class like looking at him. But, I swear, in the time I've worked with him I don't have any firsthand knowledge of him stepping over the line with anyone."

I took a step back. "Wow. You ever think about becoming a lawyer instead of a biologist?"

Cam smiled, I could see already he was going to try to deflect me again. "What do you want me to say? I'm telling you what

I know. As far as I *do* know, the guy's a looker, not a toucher. I've never seen anything inappropriate, and no one has ever told me anything different."

Ugh. That seemed like a non-answer. "Fine. I appreciate your loyalty to him and you trying to be straight with me. But can I, at least, ask you a favor? Will you come with me tonight if he wants to talk to me over dinner? I'd feel better if I wasn't alone with the guy anytime soon. Or maybe, ever."

Cam pursed his lips and nodded. "Yeah. I can do that. If it makes you feel better."

"It does. It really does. If he tries to ask you to leave, I'll tell him I want you in on the conversation too. If he *insists* that you leave, well, that'll tell me pretty much everything I need to know too."

Cam put an arm around me and turned with me back toward the trail. "Solid plan. But, you worry too much."

"You're a guy. He's heterosexual. I think my radar for stuff like this is a little more fine-tuned than yours is."

"Gotcha. I said I'd hang around if you want me to. You won't need it, but I'd be happy to. Now, how about you just focus on being happy that Flood thinks you merit attention? Seriously, Laura. That's pretty awesome news. Don't sell yourself short. It means you've impressed the hell out of him."

As we walked out of the woods and back to the cabins, Cam's enthusiasm started to rub off on me a little. Getting into the grad program at G.L.U. had been one of the main reasons I'd chosen them for my undergrad aside from the scholarship. That and it gave me the first opportunity of my life to strike out on my own. It was the first time in my almost twenty years of life I'd ever had peace and quiet. My parents were proud of me and checked in from time to time, but with a family as big as mine, it's easy to get lost in the shuffle. I relished my freedom.

"Any luck?" Flood startled me out of my head as he walked up the trail to meet us. Cam moved his hand from my shoulder abruptly and bounded ahead of me a few steps.

"Not really," Cam answered. "I'm going to check the equipment again to make sure we don't just have a bad signal. But, I'm afraid it's looking like numbers eight, two, four, and thirteen are off the grid too."

"Damn. I was really hoping for something positive today. Well, all data can be good data. It'll get us a step closer to figuring out what's affecting the mortality of this herd."

The three of us walked to the lab together. Cam went in first followed by Flood. He held the door open for me and my back stiffened as I walked by him. But, he just gave me a pleasant smile. Whatever agitation he'd had throughout the day seemed to have dissipated.

Three of the M.S.U. students were just finishing up. As soon as we walked in, they made apologies and started to pack their things.

"No rush," Flood said, his voice chipper. There was no trace of the shortness he'd directed at me earlier in the day. This Jekyll and Hyde act was wearing thin. The idea of dinner with him continued to fill me with a certain amount of dread. I hoped I was wrong or just paranoid about my concerns. I wanted to believe Cam's reassurances that Flood was a decent guy who just liked to look pretty. But, I had five brothers and a cop for a dad. They gave me a little insight into how the male mind worked sometimes. They also taught me how to take care of myself and not put up with bullshit. I was just hoping my ability to do that wouldn't also jeopardize my career path.

We finished up in the lab in relative silence. At one point, Cam walked into the cooler to store some samples, leaving Flood and me more or less alone. At first, he ignored me as he looked at slides under the microscope. I busied myself cleaning up the steel countertops and throwing away a few pairs of discarded latex gloves left behind by the other grad students.

"I think I need to have a talk with their supervising professor," Flood said as he watched me toss a stack of gloves in the waste basket.

I shrugged. "Maybe. They do kind of leave a mess around here."

"We still on for dinner?"

My heart flipped at the abruptness of his segue. "Uh. Yeah. Same as always."

He flashed a full smile. I knew he was used to that working on girls like me, but I kept my face neutral. "Relax. I won't bite you. Seriously, Laura. I've got only good things to talk to you about. You should be proud. Your family should be proud. Do you know how hard it is for me to find decent interns anymore? I hate to sound like an old fart, but I really am worried about the millennial generation."

Cam came back out of the cooler. Flood straightened and switched off the microscope.

"You guys have everything under control out here? I'd like to hit the shower before we eat. I swear I need to smell something other than deer piss for at least ten minutes."

Flood laughed. "What does it say about me that I've gotten so used to it I barely smell it anymore?"

I gave him a smile and a salute and headed out the door of the cabin. I passed a few of the Michigan State guys on the way to the showers and for a minute my heart fell. I was hoping for some solitude and mostly warm water. Luckily, by the time I got my things from my cabin and headed down there, the place was empty. I stepped around the back of the cabin. The pump had to be turned on from the outside. Once it got going, you got maybe ten minutes of warm water tops. So, I knew I needed to hurry.

I had my back to the woods as I worked the metal nozzle. It stuck sometimes, so I had to torque it hard with both hands. As I straightened, something moved in the trees to my right. Heat prickled along my spine and I stepped closer to the building, pressing my back against it. I coughed, whistled, and thumped my hand against the wooden logs that made up the outside wall, trying to make as much noise as possible as I walked back around to the front of the building.

I thought I saw a flash of gold through the trees, but nothing moved and nothing came out into full view. It was a little early for raccoons, but earlier in the week, one had tried to hop into the shower with me. Hopefully, whatever it was scampered off after the racket I made. Still, I kept one eye open as I stepped into the shower and tried to wash that woodsy smell off me as best I could.

The water felt good. Warm. At least at first. It helped me clear my head. Maybe Cam was right. I mean, for the love of God, in this day and age there's no way Byron Flood could be in the position he was if he had a history of inappropriate behavior. Was there? Maybe my five brothers and father made me extra paranoid where things like this were concerned. Still, I knew how to watch my back. Having Cam around as a buffer should solve any potential problems. Plus, I really wanted good news on the career front. Michigan was so different from northern California. I kind of loved it here. The lakes, the forests, something about it felt familiar. Like home. I could see myself living here for the rest of my life. I had yet to experience snow. I was moving into a new apartment off campus over Christmas break and was kind of hoping for one of the legendary Michigan winters Cam warned me about.

Just as the water started to turn cold, I finished. I toweled off quickly. Though I locked the door, being the only woman in a camp filled with men made me extra cautious. I threw a G.L.U. hoodie over my shoulders, laced up my Chucks, and rolled my jeans down over my ankles. The mosquitoes out here showed no mercy. I hated spraying repellant all over my freshly showered skin but had no choice if I didn't want to get eaten alive. I compromised and sprayed it mostly on my clothes.

Checking my phone, I had about fifteen minutes before dinner in the mess hall. Just enough time to stash my stuff back in my cabin and head out. I left the shower hall and darted across to my cabin. I could see lights on in the mess hall, but everything else out here was pretty quiet. In fact, Flood's Jeep was gone. I noticed as I held out the screen door to my cabin. Huh. Maybe I had more time than I thought.

I had that unsettling feeling again like something was watching me through the trees. I turned back toward the woods. Sunlight pierced through the tree tops, blinding me. I shielded my eyes but couldn't see anything. I went through the door and hooked the metal latch, locking the screen door from the inside.

I threw my towel over the wicker chair in the corner and grabbed a brush from my dresser and started the process of detangling my hair. I'd let it grow long this summer, to the middle of my back. I'd inherited my mother's thick brown locks but none of her curl. Mine hung stick straight. I flipped my head over and brushed from the nape of my neck down.

That's when I saw his shoes.

Brown hiking boots with red laces. He wore them with everything. He sat on the edge of my bed with one leg crossed over the other.

I flipped my head back over sending a shower of fat, wet droplets across the room.

"What the hell are you doing in here?" I gripped the handle of my brush as if it were a weapon.

"Relax," Flood said. He wore a smirk on his face and stared me up and down with open, naked lust. My heart thundered in my chest. I could explain away what happened the other morning. This. This was unmistakable. The asshole was in my room. He had unlocked the door. He was waiting for me.

Chapter Five

"I JUST WANTED TO TALK. I sent Cam into town for tomorrow's supplies and the other students went out to the river to collect some samples. Don't expect any of them back for a couple of hours." Flood's smile and tone didn't seem to match the naked lust I saw burning in his eyes.

"Look, I think you should go." Some part of my brain told me I should play along. Diffuse the situation. Danger signals pulsed through me. The air felt thick in my lungs as I tried to breathe.

Flood just smiled and cocked his head to the side. "I'm not going to bite you, Laura. Why are you so jumpy? I told you earlier, I wanted to talk about your future. You're talented, Laura. Capable. Bright. Ambitious. All the things this program needs. If you let me mentor you, I know you're going to do great things."

He leaned back, stretching himself out as he rested his weight on his elbows. On my fucking bed!

"Look. This just flat out isn't appropriate." I decided to go with the direct approach. Give the guy an out. "I'm not some prude and I appreciate you're taking an interest in me academically and professionally, but that is *all* I'm interested in. For now though, I need you to get out of my room."

He kept the smile on his face and tilted his chin toward me. He rose slowly from the bed and came toward me. I stepped to the side so he could get out of the cabin, my heart pounding so hard it almost hurt. I tried to keep my breath steady, not wanting to show him that I was afraid. Fear wasn't even it really, shock was more like it.

Flood reached his arm out. I thought he was going for the latch on the screen door. Instead, he grabbed my arm and jerked me toward him, his fingers digging into my upper arm.

He pulled me against him, smashing his lips down on mine. I stiffened. His tongue invaded me, he pushed me forward, angling me cruelly backward so that I nearly lost my balance. I pushed back hard, biting down on his bottom lip until I tasted blood.

Shit. Shit. Shit.

He pulled away but didn't loosen his grip on my arms. He tightened it, his fingers cutting into me hard enough I knew he'd leave bruises. I went outside of myself for an instant. This was happening. He was actually here and pushing this to a level I hadn't been prepared for.

"Fuck!" He shouted, licking his lip where the blood flowed. "Try that again and you'll be sorry."

"Get your fucking hands off me," I said. Rage made my voice low, sinister. I didn't sound like myself.

He shoved me hard toward the bed. I landed face down. Before I could scramble away, Flood was on me. He flipped me over and pressed his knees between my thighs, trying to pry them open. I brought my knee up hard, but I didn't have enough leverage to do any damage.

"You're a tease," he hissed in my face. "I know girls like you. You prance around in your tight jeans. You like the attention. Admit it."

"Go to hell, you sick freak." I pushed against him but he held me down. Some far corner of my brain even now told me this couldn't be happening. Not really. He couldn't actually be thinking of doing this to me.

"Grow up!" he said, jerking me up hard then pushing me flat against the bed again. "This is how it works, Laura. You want something from me, you gotta give a little."

"That's not how it works, asshole." I pushed against him. "That's how rape works. Is that your deal? I see you set this up perfect for yourself. Got rid of Cam."

Flood smiled. He held me down with his forearm across my chest. He took his free hand and brushed the hair out of my face. "God, you're beautiful. What the hell are you doing out here? You could be a model."

I couldn't help it. I laughed. I felt the first icy fingers of panic snake their way up my spine. It was such a ridiculous line. One more suited for someone in a seedy bar, not pinning me down ready to hurt me.

"Don't pretend you don't want this, Laura. It's me. I've seen the way you look at me. I know you wore those tight skirts in class just so I'd notice. Well, I did."

What? "No!" I shouted. "Is that what you need to hear to get it through your head? No! I don't want this. I want you to get the hell off me and get out of here. I'm going home."

He loosened his grip a little. His eyes widened as if something I'd said really did surprise him. God, could he be that delusional? Did he really think this was something I wanted?

"You go home you're finished. I'm offering you your dream shot. One recommendation from me is all you need to get into the honors program and the grad program after that."

"I said get *off* me! I don't want anything from you. Least of all this. No means no, asshole."

Flood's eyes widened again then darkened. My blood ran cold as I swear I saw a decision settle in his mind. He clenched his teeth and pressed his forearm against my chest even harder so I could barely breathe. At that moment, I understood fully. This man was capable of hurting me. Really hurting me.

"Stupid little bitch. Fine. We can play it this way too. Do you know what I can do to you? You have no idea who I am or what I can do."

He reached down and fumbled with the zipper on my jeans as I started to struggle in earnest, trying to bite, kick, claw at him any way I could. I felt his fingers digging into my waistband and pulling downward. It was then I let out a scream. It came from some deep, primal part of me, so loud Flood winced for a moment but didn't stop his advance.

He had his own jeans undone and began to pull mine down. I took a breath and screamed again. I got a hand up and managed to rake three fingers down the side of his face, drawing blood.

A growl rose behind Flood's shoulder. So deep and loud I felt it in my body as much as I heard it with my ears. Something shifted in the air around me. I saw a dark flash in the doorway, moving fast. Then, the screen buckled and tore from the door frame.

The dark wolf lunged in a great arc, its massive paws ripping into Flood's back. He never even saw it coming.

But I did.

It pulled Flood off me, sending him tumbling to the ground. He landed hard on his ass and scooted backward, pressing his back against the wall.

Flood screamed. I saw terror fill his eyes as the wolf stalked closer to him. "You can't. You fucking can't! They're gonna kill your ass so dead."

Some detached part of my brain tried to make sense of what Flood said. He was talking to the wolf as if the creature could understand him. Who were they? Who was going to kill him?

The wolf hovered over him, teeth bared, his lips curled. He snapped his jaws once and advanced on Professor Flood. I scrambled off the bed and moved toward the door. The black wolf took his eyes off Flood for a moment and turned them to me. His eyes flashed and he tilted his snout up slightly.

My world flipped upside down. In that instant, everything I worked for crumbled to dust. My arms ached from where Flood had bruised me. But, when the wolf looked at me, somehow I understood him with perfect clarity. A single thought flooded my brain.

Run!

I had the presence of mind to grab my backpack from the floor by the door. Then I burst through the ruined screen door and ran out of the cabin as fast as my feet would carry me.

Chapter Six

I TORE off toward the trail not knowing exactly where I'd go. I just knew I needed to get as far away from Byron Flood as I could. The wolf's howl rose again, sending a flash of heat through me. I wasn't scared of him. I knew I should be. What happened with Flood was horrifying. Maybe I was in shock. But the wolf. He . . . spoke to me. Not with words, but still, somehow I swore I understood him. A rational corner of my brain told me this was impossible. I was in shock. This couldn't be happening.

Even as I put distance between myself and Flood, something in me wanted to go back. I wanted to be where the wolf was. I wanted to see him again. Yet somehow, I knew what he wanted me to do. As much as I felt compelled to go to his side, I knew I had to do what he told me. Run. Get away.

I tore off down the trail, adjusting my pack on my shoulders. I still had enough daylight to make it to the ranger station before dark. I could get there. Call for help. Get on a bus. Anything to get me as far away from the camp as possible.

I don't know how long I ran. Maybe a mile. Then, as I rounded a curve, the Jeep came barreling toward me from the other direction. For a split second, I thought Flood had followed me. Then, I realized the car was coming from the wrong way. I saw Cam behind the wheel. He slammed on the brakes just before hitting me as I dove toward the trees. Mud splashed all over my jeans. Cam rolled down the window.

"Jesus! Laura! What the hell are you doing out here?"

Cam stepped out of the Jeep and helped me back to my feet. I don't know what I must have looked like to him. My damp hair hung in strings with leaves and twigs stuck in it. Beads of sweat poured down my face. His eyes widened in shock as he looked me up and down.

"What happened?"

"I'm done," I said past a dry throat.

"What?"

"Your boss is sick, Cam. He was waiting for me in my cabin as soon as you left. He tried to . . . he wanted to . . ."

God. I couldn't get the words out. How could I explain it to him? Cam just looked at me, his brow furrowed, shaking his head from side to side.

"He's a pervert all right? Straight up. Can you drive me out of here?"

"Where are you going to go?"

I lost it then. My voice rose to almost a shriek. "I don't care. Anywhere! To the ranger station. To the bus station. Anywhere Byron Flood isn't. I'm calling the fucking police, Cam. He assaulted me. If it hadn't been for . . ."

I stopped. I don't know why. But, I just couldn't bring myself to tell him about the wolf. Not yet.

"What? Why? Laura. Just hold on. What happened?"

I'd lost my temper and my patience. My blood boiled. Cam had left the Jeep running and I tried to brush past him to get to the driver's seat. Cam curled his fingers around my arm and stopped me. I winced, as he gripped me where Flood has bruised me.

"Hang on! Laura! Wait, will you?"

"I don't want to wait! I want to get as far away from this place as possible. You can either come with me or get out of the way."

Cam hesitated for a fraction of a second. He looked toward the camp, then back at me. I knew what I was asking of him. If he went with me, it wouldn't just be my academic future in the shitter. But, one way or the other, Byron Flood was done too. I didn't care what happened to me. That fucker was going down. I had the bruises on my arms to prove it.

Cam's shoulders dropped and he nodded. "Yeah. Yeah. Okay. Just get in. I'll drive you."

I let out a trembling sigh and let Cam help me into the passenger seat of the Jeep. He reached over and buckled me in. Then, he got behind the wheel and started to drive.

Except he was going the wrong way. He was heading straight back to the camp.

"Cam," I said, trying to keep my voice even. "Flood just tried to rape me. Do you understand me?" I pulled up my sleeve and showed him the bruises. The deepest ones on my upper arm were already beginning to blacken. You could clearly see the outline of four fingers and a thumbprint near my armpit.

I saw a muscle twitch near Cam's eye, but he didn't say anything. He blinked slowly and kept his eyes on the road. New dread made my blood run cold.

"Cam, turn around."

Cam just pressed his foot harder on the gas. He was going too fast for me to jump out. I smashed my fist against the side of the door.

"Cam, please turn around."

He gritted his teeth together and shot me a rage-filled look. "Just sit quiet. All you had to do was keep your mouth shut. He wouldn't hurt you."

"He *did* hurt me. That's what I'm trying to tell you. What the fuck is wrong with you?" As soon as I asked the question, I saw the answer in Cam's eyes. He wasn't my friend. He belonged to Byron Flood. His right-hand man. His protégé. I felt deeply stupid. I was completely on my own now and headed back to a place of danger.

We headed through the wooden arch over the entrance to the camp. I don't know what I expected. Cam slowed the Jeep to a crawl to avoid the large, pocked holes in the driveway made from last night's rain. I kept my eyes trained straight ahead, looking at the still open door to my cabin. The torn screen flapped in the breeze.

Cam stopped the Jeep in the center of the path separating the cabins. I just stared straight ahead at the flapping screen door to mine. Was Flood still in there? Was the wolf? Cam opened the door and started to get out.

Maybe I could still make a run for it. If the black wolf was still there, I knew he wouldn't try to hurt me, crazy as that seemed. I watched, hoping Cam would get careless and leave the keys in the ignition. Then, an unmistakable howl rose from all around us, the sound echoing off the buildings.

"What the fuck was that?"

I never had time to answer. Cam stood half in and half out of the Jeep. A silver flash came through the trees, and before I could even react, a set of jaws clamped down on Cam's arm and pulled him from the Jeep the rest of the way. It was another wolf.

Cam screamed, so did I. Blood spurted from the wound on Cam's arm and he slumped to his knees. His skin was white and waxy. It was a deep wound, but not fatal. I fumbled with my seatbelt and tried to get out. Two giant paws smacked against my window. They belonged to a different, snarling, gray wolf. His fangs glistened as he tried to break through the door and get to me.

Ahead of me, two other wolves tore out from behind the other cabins, joining in the center of the camp. Another wolf, this one bigger than the rest loped slowly around one of the cabins. He stood in the center of the camp and howled. He had golden eyes, just like my black wolf. But this one was different. He had deep red fur and when he turned to me, stone cold fear ran through me. He squared his body, turning to face me. His eyes bore straight through me.

"Laura!" Cam screamed as he held the wound on his arm. Then Cam staggered off behind one of the cabins, leaving me alone with the wolves. The gray wolf beside him looked up at me; blood covered its snout as he snapped his jaws. This one's eyes were green and filled with bloodlust. There were wolves everywhere, but I didn't see the black one. Maybe he was still with Flood.

The instant I thought it, I saw Flood stumble out of my cabin. His shirt was torn and his chest lay open with gaping wounds made from claw marks. He staggered toward the car. The rest of the wolves merely watched him go but made no move to attack him.

I tried to climb over the console and get to the driver's seat. Two wolves at the center of the camp walked toward me heading straight for the Jeep. The great red wolf, their leader, stood stoic as he watched the other members of his pack close the distance between us.

The red wolf stood frozen, staring at me, before he lifted his head and let out a howl that rent the air and speared through me. The other wolves froze and turned to him. Then they turned and stared at me. God, I understood it somehow. Me. He wanted them to go after me. The red wolf began to walk toward me slowly as the other wolves fell into step beside him.

Flood got to me first. He held his arm in front of him at an odd angle. A small bone protruded from his forearm.

"This is your fault, you bitch!" Flood gasped. Madness clouded his eyes and made his voice raise an octave higher than normal.

"Go to hell," I said, my own voice ragged.

"You're finished," he said, clutching his wrecked arm. "At the college. Everywhere. You think I'm going to let some little cocktease slut like you get away with this? You'll be lucky if expulsion is the worst thing that happens to you. This is my park. My people."

His what? I kept my eyes fixed on the approaching wolves.

Three of them advanced. The only protection I had was the Jeep, and another gray wolf pawed at the window beside me. His great claws seemed sharp enough to cut through the glass.

"That's right," Flood screamed. "I hope they rip your fucking guts out!"

Why the fuck weren't they ripping Flood's out? I got my leg out from underneath me and moved toward the driver's side. If I could just get there and get the car in gear before the rest of the pack descended on me.

Then, the wolves stopped coming. The driver's side door flew open.

"Move over." A deep voice penetrated the panic in my brain and I turned to look to its source.

He stood there, appearing out of nowhere. His broad shoulders filled the door frame. He was shirtless; a muscle at his neck twitched as he looked down at me, and those amber eyes flashed with menace. His dark hair was plastered to his forehead with sweat.

Mr. Devane. Mal.

With one swift movement, he climbed into the driver's seat and slammed the car into reverse then spun it around. The wolves charged us. There were five of them now. The red leader had joined his pack, and now each of them was hellbent on getting to me. Flood stood in the center of the camp, his body quaking with crazed laughter.

Mal downshifted and pressed the gas. The wheels spun in the mud. Everything seemed to be happening in slow motion. He swore, clenched his jaw, then gripped the gear shift hard then slammed it home. The Jeep lurched forward, rocked back, and then tires found purchase and Mal hit the gas.

I turned at last, pressing my hands against the window. I leaned my forehead against the window as the wolves broke into a run behind us.

"Buckle up!" Mal shouted. He turned to me, his eyes blazing. "They aren't going to stop until they tear you to shreds!"

Chapter Seven

MAL SKILLFULLY NAVIGATED the backwoods trail, dodging fallen branches and deep divots in the road. But, he couldn't go much faster than thirty miles an hour. It seemed painfully slow as the five wolves gave chase behind us. I chanced a look in the rearview mirror.

"They're gaining. How can they be gaining?"

Mal kept his eyes straight ahead, white-knuckling the steering wheel. He spoke through gritted teeth. "They'll have to fall back as soon as we hit pavement. If we make it that far."

Terror gripped my heart. The wolves kept coming. We passed the mile marker and the trail sign pointing to the ranger station. But, Mal veered the Jeep in the other direction toward the highway. I pressed my eyes shut, in some childish attempt to hide from the wolves. If I couldn't see them, they couldn't see me. I could pretend the last hour hadn't happened. That I hadn't nearly lost my life. My career. My friend. Fucking Cam.

I opened my eyes and looked at Mal. God, he was big. Strong.

Shirtless, his shoulders flexed as he took a hard curve, making me lurch toward him. He wore faded jeans that hugged his thigh muscles. I looked down. He was barefoot. What had he been doing alone in the woods dressed like that?

"Where are we going?"

Mal took his eyes off the road for an instant and looked at me. His amber eyes sparked as he clenched the muscles of his jaw. "I have a safe house. They can't keep up this pace for very much longer."

Mal took another sharp turn down a trail heading east. It led to nowhere. The closest paved road was a few miles in the opposite direction. Suddenly, I understood. He meant to lead the wolves on a chase until they wore out. Only then would he start for his true destination.

"Why are they after us? Where did they come from? Where did *you* come from?"

"Later," Mal said. "Let's just focus on losing them."

I nodded and checked the side mirror. Sure enough, the pack began to lose ground. They still followed, but they'd dropped back a few yards. Mal pressed the gas as hard as he dared. A low-hanging branch slammed against my door, startling me.

"Hang on," Mal said. "There's a sharp turn coming up. I don't want to slow down."

I gripped the dashboard and braced my feet on the floor. Mal jerked the wheel hard right. The wheels spun, and for an instant, I thought we would tip. But, Mal executed the turn and pressed the accelerator again, taking the Jeep up to almost forty.

We drove through the trails like that for a few more minutes.

Mal took so many turns I knew he had to have circled back at least once. I'd gotten hopelessly lost and hoped he knew where he was going. He seemed to. Then finally, when I felt brave enough to turn and look, the wolves were gone. I heard a plaintive howl; turning to Mal, I saw the hairs raise on the back of his neck. He kept his eyes on the road and his fists gripped the steering wheel. He made one more turn, and the dirt trail beneath our tires gave way to gravel. We were headed toward the highway.

I let out a breath I hadn't realized I'd been holding. Mal turned on the headlights. A mile marker appeared, indicating we were just three miles from the nearest town. For the first time, I felt my heart begin to slow. We'd made it. Or, we'd almost made it.

Mal made the turn onto the highway and I could almost breathe normally again. Though my hands shook as I raised them to pull the zipper on my hoodie. Full night now, a chill ran through me. He drove for a few miles, then took an exit back toward the forest.

"We're almost there," he said. "When we stop, stay in the car for a minute until I make sure it's clear."

"Okay."

Mal turned down a dirt road deeper into the woods. He parked the Jeep beside a big oak tree and got out. Its occupant, a pissed off owl, hooted in protest. Mal got out of the Jeep and put his finger to his lips motioning me to keep quiet.

He rounded the front of the Jeep and disappeared into the brush. My heart started to pound again. I was alone in the woods, far from anyplace I knew, with a virtual stranger. I should have been terrified, and I was. But somehow, I trusted Mal to keep me safe. That said, I wasn't an idiot. I unbuckled my seatbelt and crawled over the seat to get to the back of the Jeep.

Flood kept supplies under a tarp behind the passenger seats. I lifted the corner and felt along the floor. The moon provided a little natural light, and I was afraid to switch on the interior lights. I found a flashlight, a canteen. I stuffed that into my backpack and kept looking. My fingers closed around the cold metal barrel of his 12 gauge shotgun. The one he'd used to shoot at the black wolf the other day.

"Gotcha!" I whispered. I pulled the gun over the seat and laid it flat. I felt around on the floor. He had a small box of ammo. Twelve rounds. Hopefully, I wouldn't need any of it, but there was no point in leaving it behind. I shoved that in my backpack, grabbed the shotgun, and crawled back over into front passenger seat to wait for Mal.

He came through the thick of the trees. The moonlight caught his eyes, making them glow a familiar gold that sent a ripple of fear and recognition through me. I shook it off. My eyes were playing tricks on me. It had been a rough hour and a half.

"Come on," he said, coming around to the passenger side he opened my door. He gave me no more than a slight eyebrow raise when he saw the shotgun in my hand. "We need to get inside. You sure you can handle that thing without shooting yourself in the foot?"

I slung it over my shoulder. "I'm sure. You got a problem with me taking it?"

Mal shrugged and shook his head. "No ma'am. As long as it doesn't slow you down."

With that, he turned and headed into the thick of the trees. He didn't order me to follow him. I could have turned around and gotten back in the Jeep. Maybe that was the wisest choice. And yet, as Mal's silhouette in the moonlight got farther away, my heart raced. A different kind of panic rose in me as the distance between us widened. Before I could even process the thought, I took a hesitant step toward him. Then another. I left the Jeep and everything familiar to me as I followed Mal Devane deeper into the woods.

Chapter Eight

WE WALKED FOR ALMOST AN HOUR. The forest grew thick around us. No trails marked the way, but Mal knew exactly where he was going. I had to practically run to keep up with him with his long, powerful strides. He looked back to make sure I was there but otherwise didn't stop. It seemed like a test. Could I handle myself with him? God. None of it made sense. I'd been operating on nothing but base instinct since Byron Flood attacked me. And though I couldn't explain it, it *mattered* that Mal knew I could handle myself.

Finally, we made it to another clearing. At the center, another log cabin much like those back at the G.L.U. outpost, but I'd never seen this one before. We were still in Manistee Forest, but as far as I knew, this place wasn't charted on any of the maps.

"It's mine," Mal said though I hadn't voiced my question. "Or at least, it is now. We should be safe enough for the night. The pack's lost the scent by now. They'll retreat until morning."

Mal opened the door of the cabin and walked inside. I followed. He shut it and latched it behind us, leaving us in total darkness. Blind, I could somehow still sense Mal as he moved deeper into the room. He fumbled with something then a propane lantern flared to life, casting ghostly shadows across his face.

The cabin was simple. One rectangular room with a bed and blankets on one side, a fireplace in the center, and a kitchen on the other side with a coal burning stove and a sink.

"Running water from a well out back," Mal said. "Sorry, that's the most luxurious thing I've got out here."

"Thank you," I said, and the room got quiet. He knew I wasn't talking about the cabin's accommodations. He didn't know me. He owed me nothing. But, he'd very likely saved my life back there and risked his own to bring me here.

Mal raised a brow and nodded. I noticed the cut above his eye again. Fresh blood oozed from the corner of it. He must have scraped it against a branch or something while we walked. It didn't seem to bother him as he set the lantern on a stone ledge above the fireplace. He grabbed another one from against the wall and lit it, casting the cabin in warm, flickering orange light.

He stood there for a moment regarding me. His eyes glinted as he towered over me. I hadn't looked at him before. Not this close. Not this way. Dark stubble peppered his square jaw. I wondered what it would feel like brushing against my skin. As soon as the thought entered my mind, heat flashed through me and took my breath away.

"Are you all right?" He kept his deep voice low, barely above a whisper. Still, the sound of it vibrated in my ears.

I looked behind me. The only furnishings in the room were the bed and two cane chairs against the wall. I grabbed one of those and pulled it into the center of the room. My knees felt weak all of a sudden. This was the first moment I'd had to take a breath since everything started. I sank slowly into the chair.

"Where did you come from? I mean, what were you doing at the camp?"

Something flickered behind Mal's eyes. He rested one arm on the stone mantel and brushed his chin with his fingers as he considered my question. Then, he looked back at me, his eyes boring straight through me hard enough to make me shudder.

"Did he hurt you?"

He? My breath hitched as my mind flashed to the gray wolf as he tried to claw his way through the passenger door and get to me. "No," I finally said. "It just scared me. I mean, you saw. It never even touched me."

Then, I finally lost it. A lump traveled from low in my gut and settled in my throat. Tears welled in my eyes and I knew I'd go very near the edge of hysteria if I started crying now. But, I couldn't help it. Flood would have hurt me, really hurt me. Cam was supposed to be my friend, and his betrayal stung the most. He led me back to that asshole like he meant to serve me up to him like dessert. Then there were the wolves. Except for the black wolf, they meant to tear me apart. There was no mistaking that. I couldn't help the dark thoughts that rose up within me as I fantasized about the lethal force the black wolf used to tear Flood off of me.

"What made them do that?" I said. I drew my knees up and hugged them, knowing full well what I must look like to Mal, huddled in that chair like that. He came to me, kneeled down on one knee and put a hand on my shoulder. His touch seared me and made me jolt.

"What's your name?" he said, that deep timbre of his voice skittering across my skin. "I don't even know it."

"What? Oh, right. It's Laura. Laura Prince."

A smirk lifted his mouth and he brought his hand up and ran the pad of his thumb across my forehead. "Princess, huh? Seems fitting."

I choked back a sob and it came out as an undignified snort. "Prince. I'm nobody's princess."

Mal shrugged and rose. "We'll see about that. In the meantime, Princess. Why don't you try and get some sleep? You've had a long day. I'll take you back to civilization in the morning."

The air seemed to go out of my lungs. Shit. It had to be the trauma of the day. I wasn't myself. But, the idea of Mal taking me anywhere that wasn't where he was filled me with cold fear. I flat out didn't want to leave his side. It made no sense. He was a stranger. I'd just been through so much I latched on to the first person who acted like a human being.

"Take the bed."

"What about you?"

Mal stood near the door. He cocked his head to the side as he regarded me. "I don't need much sleep. Not tonight anyway. I want to do a sweep, make sure they didn't pick up the scent."

Fear shot through me, making my heart race again. "I don't understand it. Why did those wolves attack like that? Why did they chase us? Why weren't they attacking Cam or anyone else at the camp?"

Mal blew out a breath. His eyes fixed on some point over my head. This was the second time I'd watched him pause like that before answering my question. It made me angry this time. He knew far more about what was going on than he seemed willing to tell me.

"Look," I said rising. I took a step toward him. "What happened back there wasn't normal. I'm no expert, but I know wolves don't behave like that. And they don't belong this far south. And I believed you when you said those fuckers were after me next. I know it sounds strange, but I could see it in their eyes. They wanted to rip my throat out. Why? And how the hell did you know to come out there? You're half-dressed and in bare feet. Why didn't they rip *your* throat out?"

Mal clenched his jaw hard. I didn't mean to snap at him. I was grateful for what he'd done. But, at that moment, panic, fatigue, maybe a little post-traumatic stress . . . all of it won out,, leaving me quaking with rage. I wanted answers. I wanted everything that happened in the last hour to make sense. This man knew something. He didn't belong in the camp. He just happened to be there when everything turned upside down. As I thought it, fresh panic crept through me, spreading icy tentacles across my spine.

"Just go to sleep, Princess," he said. I reeled back from his words as if he'd slapped me. What the ever loving fuck?

Then, Mal's face softened as he sensed the rage and indignation boiling to the surface in me. He took a step forward and placed his hands on my upper arms. His touch was gentle but I winced. My tender skin ached where Professor Flood had bruised me.

Something passed through Mal's eyes. A muscle twitched in his temple.

"Show me," he said, his voice dark with menace.

"What?"

"Show me where he hurt you."

I took a step back, but Mal kept his hands on me with a firm but gentle grip.

"I'm fine."

"I won't ask you again. Show me."

I jerked myself away from him. It was in me to protest. It was none of his business. But, the way Mal looked at me, his eyes filled with equal parts rage and concern, my heart cracked down the middle and I didn't want to deny him anything. Something powerful was happening inside me as I stood in that room with him. I didn't understand it. I knew I should probably be afraid of it. But, I wanted nothing more than to give in to it.

Slowly, I unzipped my hoodie and pulled my arms out of the sleeves. Underneath, I wore a thin, white tank top. Cool air brushed across my skin, raising gooseflesh on my arms. I shuddered. Mal stepped closer, holding one of the lanterns in his hands. He closed his fingers around the elbow of my right arm and gently lifted it so he could see the deep, purple bruises covering my upper arm. They formed the perfect outline of Flood's hands. The bruise on my left arm was even worse, mottled black and green.

Mal's whole body went rigid as his eyes darted over my marred skin. His jaw quaked as he ground his teeth together. A low rumbling came from his throat that sounded primal, animalistic.

"It could have been worse," I finally said, trying to break the tension. Mal didn't take his eyes off the bruises. "He wanted to . . ."

Before I could finish, Mal looked at me. "You think I don't know what he wanted? I could fucking smell it on him. I never should have let you go back to that place with him. I'm sorry I didn't get there faster."

"What are you talking about? How could you?" Then, I remembered Mal's warning when I first met him at the general store. Was he trying to tell me he could sense Flood's intentions even then?

I took a step back and this time, Mal let me go. I wanted to ask him a million other questions, but something in his face, his posture, made me stop. "Just try and get some sleep," he said, his voice softer, calmer now. It made me calmer too. I couldn't explain it, but it was like his moods affected mine. Was I so traumatized that I couldn't even regulate my own emotions? The idea of that unsettled me almost as much as everything else that happened today.

"I'll keep watch," he said. "I swear. Nothing's getting near you tonight. You're safe."

I nodded. Suddenly, the need for sleep became so powerful, I think I might have dropped right there if the bed weren't so close. I went to it, crawling to the head. The mattress was firm. A soft down comforter covered it, and all I wanted to do was sink into the thing and disappear for a few hours. I kicked off my shoes and pulled the covers around me, already overcome with drowsiness.

"You can take the shotgun," I said, yawning and pointing to where I'd leaned it against the wall.

Mal gripped the doorknob and watched me as I settled under the covers. "Thanks, but I'm deadlier without it."

Chapter Nine

I DREAMT the black wolf came to me in the predawn hours. He stood at the foot of the bed watching me, those familiar golden eyes flashing. I reached out and placed a hand on his great head. He whined, pressed his ears flat, and put his paws on the mattress, making the bed sink to one side. He sniffed the air and his nose went to my upper arm. A low growl made my body vibrate as he licked the worst of the bruises, sending waves of soothing heat through me.

He'd been there that night. He knew what Flood tried to do to me. He came to protect me. Somehow, I knew he belonged to me. Or that I belonged to him. Then, sun stabbed through the window, warming my skin. When I opened my eyes, the wolf was gone and I knew I'd dreamt the whole thing.

But, Mal was gone too. A mourning dove sang right outside the window and a breeze picked up, rustling through the trees. I'd slept like the dead and woke with my head clear. Mal had been right. I needed sleep more than anything else. Now though, I needed a toothbrush.

I startled when the door to the cabin creaked open. Mal stepped inside. With the sun behind him, for an instant I saw nothing more than a great, black shadow. Then, he closed the door and came to me.

"All quiet out there?" My voice was groggy with sleep and I cleared my throat.

Mal nodded. He'd changed. He wore a fresh pair of jeans, hiking boots, and a white t-shirt that stretched taut across his biceps. He pointed to a small table by the bed.

"I keep some hotel-sized supplies in there. Toothbrush, soap. That kind of thing. You can use the pump well outside if you need to. It's potable. Don't be afraid to drink it."

"Oh, God bless you!" I said, throwing the covers off me. I took what I needed from the drawer and headed for the door.

"Breakfast when you get back," he said. "Nothing fancy. I've got trail mix bars and some fresh fruit." He seemed to have my body trained to his voice because my stomach let out an audible growl.

I shot him a sheepish grin and went out the door. A light fog settled over the treetops and cool air raised the hairs on my arms. I found the red pump in the back of the cabin. Despite the sulfur smell, the water was cool going down. The bruises on my arms had deepened to an ugly black on both sides. God, in the heat of the moment, I hadn't realized how rough Flood had actually been. He could have wrapped those hands around my neck and choked the life out of me.

My knees went a little weak at the thought of it. I splashed more cool water on the back of my neck. As I washed some of the grime and sweat away from the night before, a new clarity filled my head. I had to get back. Over the last few hours, this cabin had provided a little bubble of protection against all the ugliness that had happened. But, I had to face it. I had to call the university and file a report. I couldn't let that asshole ruin my academic career as he'd threatened. If he'd pulled that shit with me, he had to have a pattern of doing it. I couldn't let this get swept under the rug or he might try it with another girl. The wolves had to be gone by now.

I reached down to cup my hand under the water. My knuckle scraped against a sharp piece of metal at the base of the thing, slicing the skin open. It wasn't a deep cut, but it stung and the blood flowed freely.

"Shit," I muttered. I ran my hand under the water to clean it out. I hoped Mal had some bandages stashed somewhere along with the trail mix bars and hotel soaps.

Sucking on my finger, I headed back into the cabin. Mal had already made the bed and pointed to the kitchen counter where he'd laid out the food such as it was.

"Do you happen to have a first aid kit somewhere? I sliced my finger on the pump. It's not deep but I need to stop the bleeding. Come to think of it, why don't you let me have a look at that cut above your eye? I noticed you reopened it last night."

Mal reached under the bed and pulled out a brown paper bag and dumped its contents on the bed. It was gauze, the bottle of iodine, and the bandages I'd given him at the store the other day.

"See? I told you those would come in handy. Have a seat," I said, pointing to one of the cane chairs. "My turn to take care of you."

Mal let out a noise that was part growl and part laugh. I smiled as he handed me the basket. I pulled out two lengths of gauze and medical tape and set one on the other chair. I wrapped the other quickly around my own finger. Then, I took a cotton ball and dipped it in the iodine.

"You never said how you got that," I said as I pressed the cotton ball to his cut. On closer inspection, it wasn't really a cut. Not a clean one anyway. It looked more like something had taken a chunk of out of him.

Mal hissed through his teeth when the iodine touched his skin. "Don't be a baby," I teased him.

"Be careful, Princess," he said. "I bite."

He was teasing, but his tone sent a flash of heat through me. I pulled my hand away for an instant. Shaking my head against my newly jittery nerves, I pressed my finger against his forehead again. I was careless though. The gauze around my own finger came loose and a drop of blood fell, as I pressed my finger against Mal's cut. So careless. Our blood mixed. I was about to make a joke about what a shitty a nurse I'd make.

But, then the world fell away.

Heat. Light. Sound. Blood coursed through my veins. My own heartbeat filled my ears, joined by another even stronger one. For an instant, I wasn't me. Or at least, I didn't see as me. Every sense sharpened. The scent of pungent, rotting leaves just outside the door filled me. I heard the footfall of some creature moving softly through the woods. A rabbit.

Then there was Mal. His eyes changed, flaming bright. The pupils widened, and the amber flecks spread, taking over the whites of his eyes. He growled low and gripped my wrist. Whatever happened to me, something similar happened to him. He was *in* me somehow. It was like I saw myself through

Mal's eyes. Heat rose on my own skin, making it glow. His heartbeat filled me, became part of me, if only for an instant.

Then, I pulled away. Mal dropped his grip on my arm as I staggered backward.

"What was that? Who . . . what are you?"

I don't even know who asked the question. I ended up with my back pressed against the far wall before I sank down to the ground. Mal rose and loomed over me. His eyes flashed again. I squeezed mine shut tight. When I opened them again, Mal's eyes were normal but filled with menace.

His whole body rippled and quaked. Beads of sweat formed at his temples.

"Go," he said, his voice barely sounding human as he tried to contain whatever made him tremble. "Now. Don't look back."

And again, when Mal gave a command, my body felt compelled to follow it. My heart beat nearly out of my chest as I found the strength to get to my feet. I grabbed my pack by the door and the shotgun.

Then, I ran outside and didn't dare look back.

Chapter Ten

EAST. I think I needed to go east. The Jeep would be there, parked just where Mal left it. My heart beat nearly in my throat as I ran as fast as my legs would carry me. I slung the shotgun over my shoulder and watched the trail in front of me. I couldn't afford to fall. Not now.

Getting to safety. Getting far away from this cursed forest and whatever hell lived in it. That was the only thing that mattered. And yet, it seemed like I might be running from it for the rest of my life.

I took a wrong turn. The forest closed in around me. My ankles became ensnared in thick weeds. Panting, I pulled one foot out, then the other. The trees seemed to spin around me, making me dizzy, disoriented. I couldn't get my bearings. This *had* to be the right way. I lunged forward until I found my footing again. Blood coursed through me as I tried to put distance between myself and the cabin. And Mal. Oh, God. Mal. With each step I took, stabbing pain tore through my chest. I wanted to go back. I wanted to run. It was like I didn't know myself anymore.

I burst into a small clearing and stopped. I put my hands on my knees and took a deep breath, trying to quiet the clanging in my ears. Panic would not help me now. It was broad daylight. I had a shotgun and I knew how to use it. The Jeep and a country road were not that far away.

Finally, my pulse started to slow and the fog lifted from my brain. I straightened my back and looked toward the sky. The sun rose to my left. I'd been heading the right way. I blew a breath out hard. I set the gun down and threaded my arms through the loops of my backpack, evenly distributing the weight of it. Then, I reached down, grabbed the gun, and took my first sure step since fleeing the cabin.

I never had a chance to take a second.

The black wolf burst through the trees near my right shoulder and stood beside me. He held his thick, black tail high and took a slow step forward. I raised the shotgun, jamming the butt against my shoulder. At this range, I could blow its head clean off.

Time slowed then seemed to stop altogether as I kept the shotgun aimed at the wolf and he stood before me, unblinking. He let out a low, rumbling growl that seemed to move through my whole body.

He took another step forward, his golden eyes flashing with intelligence. Blood crusted just above his left eye where Flood's bullet had ricocheted. Recognition slammed into my brain and my finger trembled over the trigger. My breath left my lungs and my blood heated.

The black wolf raised his head just a fraction of an inch. I knew him. Knew those eyes. He came to me in my dreams. He came to me when I needed him most. Some rational part of my brain told me I must be going crazy. Except I wasn't. As we stood there in the middle of the woods in some strange stalemate, everything I believed about the world shifted. I don't remember lowering the shotgun. But, all of a sudden it was on the ground beside me and it was my turn to take a step forward. My backpack slid off my shoulders and I let that drop too. I held out my hand, my fingers shaking as I reached for the wolf.

A rumbling sound came from within him. He reared up on his hind legs while his fur rolled and his bones shifted inside of him, stretching, pulling, his front paws drew up and reached out for me. Then, he touched me, but his paw was gone. In its place, a strong hand with tanned flesh and a fine dusting of dark hair trailing up his arm. The wolf was gone and Mal stood before me, naked, strong, powerful.

I shuddered as he threaded his fingers through my hair, tilting my head back as he looked down at me. His golden eyes still had more wolf in them than man. Dark desire flared deep inside me. I wasn't afraid. I knew this. Knew him. I belonged here, even though I knew it was impossible.

"Who are you?" he whispered.

I never got to answer. Mal lowered his head and pressed his lips against mine. I melted into him. As he kissed me, he poured warmth, strength, and power into me. I reached up and slid my hands across his chest, his broad shoulders. I wanted to know every line of his body, every cord of muscle. I hungered for him in a way that shocked me. But, as he kept on kissing me, ran his hand down my back and pulled me even closer to him, I knew that I had to have him. All of him. Now.

Before I could even think, I reached down and fumbled with the button of my jeans and tugged them down. Mal lifted the hem of my t-shirt and pulled it over my head. Just that fraction of a second when I had to stop kissing him to get the thing off seemed too long. He took a step back, and his eyes sparked as he watched me. I wriggled the rest of the way out of my jeans and stood before him wearing nothing but my black bra and panties.

He waited. A slow smile spread across his lips, swollen from kissing. Heat flared between my legs more primal than anything I'd ever known. I'd almost lost the ability to form thoughts except for *this . . . yes . . . his.*

Gasping, I reached back and unhooked my bra, letting it fall to the ground. My breasts swung free. As Mal watched me, I couldn't take my eyes off his perfect form. Chiseled muscle and sinew, a dark trail of hair ran down his rippled abdomen. My eyes followed it as I took in the sight of him. His cock swung huge and hard before me. I couldn't help startling a bit at the size of it. He was thick and long and perfect.

My own sex throbbed as I hooked a thumb into the waistband of my panties and shed those too. Then, Mal was done looking. He needed to touch me again as much as I needed him. He whispered my name against my temple as his fingers played across the small of my back then cupped my ass and drew me to him.

We ended up on the ground together. He didn't have to tell me what to do; my body was tuned to his already. He had me on my back in a fresh pile of leaves, the tall maples forming a canopy above us. I drew my knees up and spread them wide, offering myself to him like some wild, wanton, shameless thing. Right then, it's what I was. All I wanted to be.

Mal positioned himself between my thighs. He drew a single finger down between my breasts. My breath hitched and I quivered as he slid that finger slowly down over the slope of my stomach, over my bellybutton then all the way down. He tapped my poor, swollen clit with his fingertip. Just that light touch, that tiny motion made the heat between my legs peak and a gush of juices trickled down as if he'd commanded it. On an instinctual level I knew he could. Oh, God, he could. Just the slightest touch, the crook of his finger and my body seemed to respond instantly. I knew I should be shocked at how ready I was for him. But I wasn't. Instead, I found myself arching my back, spreading my legs even wider in offering.

This. Always this. I wanted him to fill me, claim me, own me. Nothing else that ever happened before or would happen after seemed to matter in that instant. There was just now, the heat between my legs, the hard length of Mal's erection as he pressed himself against my thigh.

Then, Mal pressed my knees flat against the ground, spreading me impossibly wide. He settled himself between my thighs and lowered his head. A single flick of his tongue seemed to send stars shooting across the sky.

"Please!" I begged him once and knew it was just the beginning. I would do anything just to have him touch me like that again. And he did. He took two fingers and spread me wide, exposing my sensitive little bud for his inspection. Just the slightest kiss of air across that tight bundle of nerves had me writhing for him, stretching myself, struggling to spread myself even wider.

He kissed me there, sending a jolt of electricity through me to the roots of my hair. I bucked and thrust before him, tearing at the ground as he teased and coaxed me with his skillful tongue and fingers to the edge of desire and madness.

"God, oh God. Please."

"Say it," he said, his voice low and deep.

"Yes. Please!"

"Say it!"

His voice made the tiny hairs on the back of my neck raise as he commanded me. I would do anything for him. I could belong to him. And then I knew exactly what he wanted and I gave it to him.

"Yes. I'm yours. I need you. Please."

Mal drew himself up, kneeling before me as he stroked the thick length of his cock. God. He seemed even bigger, harder than before. He worked himself up and down and I swear my mouth watered at the sight of it. I wanted him deep inside me. I wanted to taste him, tease him with my mouth and tongue the way he'd done to me.

Mal positioned himself between my legs and put a steadying hand on my shoulder. He didn't have to say it. I knew to grab my knees and keep them spread wide so he could ease himself into me. I gasped and shuddered as I felt the tip of him brush against my hungry, waiting sex. I was so wet, so ready. Even so, my eyes went wide as I felt the first slow push as he entered me. He was so big I thought he might tear me apart.

His eyes glinted gold as he guided himself in the rest of the way. I felt a tiny, stinging stab of pain as he stretched me. But then it gave way to exquisite pleasure unlike anything I'd known. He fit me and filled me completely as if I were made just for him.

I arched my back and wrapped my legs around his hips. Mal put his hands on my shoulders and looked down at me, blocking out the sun behind him. At that moment, I knew it's what he was. My sun. My moon. My everything. As he began the first slow thrusts inside me, it was like I came alive for the first time. The grass beneath me, the trees above, even the timid creatures around us seemed part of him. Part of me.

Mal started slow, but only for a moment. Before long, instinct took hold and he began to fuck me hard and deep. I kept my legs wrapped around him and held on as he pressed himself into me, filling every corner of my being. The first slow build of desire washed over me. I gripped Mal's shoulders and hung on. My fingers dug into his back. I drew blood, but that only seemed to spur him on. His eyes flashed from man to wolf and back again. I leaned up and brought my lips to his. He kissed me hard and deep, devouring me body and soul.

Then finally, I felt him tense. His balls seized beneath me and he let go. He came deep inside me, filling me with his seed as I squeezed my legs around him tighter to contain it. Careless. Reckless maybe. But I couldn't stop. I hungered for him in a way I'd never known before.

As Mal began to crest down, he pulled out of me. For an instant, I felt empty and bereft. But Mal slid his hands under my back and flipped me. I got my hands out in front of me as he angled my hips, raising them backward to get me in position. I knelt on all fours, pressing my chin against my hands, spreading my legs as wide as I could. And he entered me again. Not slowly this time, but rough and strong. My teeth rattled as he pumped the rest of his seed into me. He squeezed my ass with one hand and reached around with the other, finding my sex again. As he came, he worked me until my thighs quaked. My knees buckled as I tried to lay flat. I had no strength left. But, Mal would have none of that. He kept a strong hand on my hip, holding me in position with my ass high in the air. He coaxed my orgasm out of me. I threw my head back, my hair arcing behind me as Mal rode me. Each pulse of ecstasy rippled through me, wave after delicious wave. I came hard and deep as Mal kept himself inside me. My walls clenched around him, milking the last drop of seed from him.

Then, when he knew he'd wrung every ounce of pleasure out of me, he finally withdrew. He pulled me against him, cradling my head and hooking his hands under my knees. I was glad for it because I didn't think I'd be able to walk. I didn't have to. Mal stood and carried me back toward the cabin.

Chapter Eleven

I COULDN'T STOP TOUCHING him. Mal became a different kind of sustenance, but one my body craved just as much as food or air. We sat on the edge of the bed together. I held my hand on his knee or cupped his face or ran my fingers across his back tracing the lines I'd made when I scratched him. He was already starting to heal.

"I knew," I said much later when I regained the ability to form words. "I can't explain it, but I think I knew from that first moment when you came to me in the woods. The wolf was you."

Mal nodded. I reveled in the wonder of his body. The broadness of his back. His thick, dark hair almost the same shade as mine. I laid a lock of mine across his shoulder. They were nearly a perfect match. Had that always been the case? I hadn't noticed until now. I felt drunk from him. Woozy. But Mal remained stoic. Lines of worry creased his brow when all I felt was contentment.

"What is it?" I finally asked. I laid back on the bed on my side.

I was naked still. So was he. It felt natural, like we'd been together forever.

"I should have let you leave. I shouldn't have gone after you."

My heart fluttered with the first waves of fear. I sat up. Would he ask me to leave now? Could I? I knew what was happening to me . . . between *us* was strange. Supernatural. But it felt real and strong and the thought of leaving him made my blood run cold. I should be scared. Terrified. Mal was an honest to God werewolf. I should be panicking. Running screaming through the woods. And yet, it seemed the most natural thing in the world. As odd as that sounds, knowing the truth made the world make more sense to me, not less.

"Do you want me to leave now?" The idea filled me with dread, but I hadn't taken complete leave of my senses. I'd just had the greatest fuck of my life and kind of hoped it wouldn't be the last, but it couldn't be enough to make me chuck my whole future away. I still had to deal with Flood.

"You won't be safe with me forever," he said. Mal rose off the bed and grabbed his jeans off the floor. He tossed mine to me. They landed on the pillow near my head. "The pack isn't going to stop looking for me, and I can't stop looking for them. You asked me why they didn't come after me yesterday. It's only because I was lucky enough to be faster for a second. And they didn't expect me to shift. Next time, it's going to be much, much worse."

Mal zipped his pants and ran a hand across the stubble on his chin. "Get dressed," he said. "I'm going to take you out of here."

"Where do you want me to go?"

"Anywhere that's far away from me. Preferably on a plane

headed in the other direction. Where's home for you? Your real home?"

I let out a sigh and thrust my foot into the leg of my jeans. I hopped on one foot to get them up past my hips then grabbed my shirt. My bra was still out in the woods somewhere. "Northern California."

"Perfect," he said. "Go back there. Never come back here."

My blood boiled. Mal tore through the cabin until he found the keys to the Jeep. He went to the front door and threw it open. Rage started to simmer in me. It seemed being around Mal Devane sparked extreme emotions in me one way or another. But for now, who the hell did he think he was ordering me around? I didn't ask him to inject himself into my life. He had no right to tell me how to live it.

"I live here now. I go to school here. I'm not throwing everything away I've worked for because of Byron Flood or a wild pack of wolves. And certainly not until I understand just what the fuck is going on." I grabbed the edge of the door, pulled it out of Mal's hands and slammed it shut. I crossed my arms in front of me, took a wide stance, and stared him down.

A spark went through Mal's eyes that sent a wave of heat straight down my spine and settled between my legs. Good God. I needed to quit thinking with my libido where he was concerned. I wanted answers. Now. I turned on my heel and sat down on one of cane chairs. I gestured to the other with my chin. "Talk."

Mal narrowed his eyes at me and let out a chuff that sounded pure wolf. He didn't sit. Instead, he paced. I wanted to stay mad at him. I found it difficult to concentrate as he walked in front of me shirtless.

"The pack. They're like you?" I asked.

Mal stopped mid-stride and turned toward me. "They're were. Yes."

"Are they your pack?"

Mal's eyes flashed. "No. I don't have a pack. Not anymore."

I sensed pain in his voice as he said it. It cut through me, leaving a hollow space. I wanted to go to him and ease it. But, Mal wasn't finished.

"The pack I came from lives up north. The Wild Lake lands at the tip of the lower peninsula, spreading through the upper peninsula and into Canada."

"Why aren't they here with you?"

Mal stood in front of the fireplace, resting his elbow on the stone mantle. He rubbed his chin between his fingers. "I've been exiled."

He said it with a finality that tore at my heart. Exile. Mal was part wolf. I knew what that had to mean for someone like him. He was all alone when he should be part of a pack. Again, I wanted to go to him but knew on instinct he needed space if he was going to get through this.

"The large red wolf," he continued. "The one who called to the others back at your camp. His name is Asher. He's their Alpha. He started a war with the Wild Lake packs long ago. Now he's back trying to finish it. He wants to take over the lands we have in Michigan. He wants revenge for things he thinks we took from him. He won't stop until he's killed every last one of us."

Asher. The red wolf. Just as recognition slammed into my brain when I saw Mal as the wolf, I realized I knew Asher too. He'd been the man I saw arguing with Flood the other day. My head spun as I tried to sort out what it all meant. I shook my head and looked back at Mal.

"Then why are you the only one who's fighting him? I counted five of them including that big one. How many others are there in Wild Lake? Whether you're exiled or not, you just said Asher's after the other wolves from Wild Lake. Why aren't they down here fighting by your side?"

Mal pressed his fist against the mantle. "I told you. I'm in exile. Asher is mine to bring down. The rest of his pack . . . they belong at Wild Lake too. It's my job to free them from Asher and bring them back home. If they'll follow me."

"If they'll . . . uh . . . last I saw, they were trying to rip my face off. Yours too. What makes you think they want to go?"

"Asher's their Alpha. They do what he commands. If given the chance to decide for themselves, I believe they'll come with me. It's Asher who wants me dead along with anyone who's close to me."

A lump settled in my throat as his words sank in.

"I'm sorry," Mal turned toward me, pain filling his eyes. "I shouldn't have brought you here. And now you know why you have to go. I've made a mistake where you're concerned. As long as you're here, you're a way for Asher to get to me. If he finds you, he'll use you against me. He'll have no qualms about hurting you either. Badly. You don't belong in the middle of this fight."

But, I wasn't the only one in the middle of it. Everything had happened so fast. Seemed so incredible at the time. But, Flood, Cam, they weren't afraid of the gray wolves. Flood had some kind of relationship with Asher.

"What's Flood's part in this? He knows Asher's pack, doesn't he? He's connected to them somehow."

Mal clenched his jaw. "Yes. He must be a friend of the pack. I suspected it the first time I laid eyes on him. I could *smell* Asher on him. It means they were in the same room together not long before I saw him at the store with you. And that's what I mean. Just that little bit of contact was enough for me to sense Asher. With the time we've spent together, he can track you the same way. I don't know what Flood and Asher's relationship is or what Flood's getting out of it. But, Asher and his pack need a lot of lands to hunt while they're here. A sort of home base. It would make sense that he'd have someone connected with either the rangers or your outpost watching out for the pack."

I nodded. Quickly as I could, I recounted what I remembered about the argument Flood and Asher had. "They were talking about you only I didn't realize it at the time. And Flood said something about helping to keep the rangers off Asher's back. So, he does that and Asher basically agrees not to rip Flood's throat out?"

Mal nodded. "If I were in Asher's place, it's what I'd do. We're strong, but we're vulnerable this far south. The pack needs a safe haven, and it looks like Flood's helping to provide it."

"Now I get why Flood tried to blow me off after that day in the woods when he shot at you. Told me I was seeing things. That you were a coyote."

Mal scoffed and started pacing again. "There's only five of them, but even a pack that size can't sustain themselves in a place like this without drawing attention. We have outposts of our own down here, but Asher's had help from some packs down in Kentucky and we've had to abandon them. In addition to his vendetta against the Wild Lake packs, he wants to claim lands all through Michigan. It looks like he thinks he's got a foothold in Manistee now."

"Why were you exiled?"

Mal stopped pacing. He clenched his fists at his side. "It's a long story."

"Give me the highlights."

"I was born an Alpha. There wasn't room for two of us in my pack. I made a challenge. I lost. The Alpha I challenged could have killed me. It would have been his right. But, someone intervened on my behalf. Some of the wolves in Asher's pack are very important to the people in Wild Lake. I've been given a chance to bring them back and claim my place among the Wild Lake packs for good."

I raised a brow. "That's a pretty simple story, Mal. So now you're down here trying to claim a pack of your own. I get it. What can I do to help?"

Mal took a step back. He looked at me as if I'd grown a third eye. "Why would you want to help me?"

I stood up and went to him. "I have no idea. I really don't. Except that fucker Asher sicked those wolves on me. I was there. They had a kind of bloodlust. And if they're working with Flood, all the more reason to hate them. I'm not one to uh . . . pardon the pun . . . . turn tail from a fight. Flood's going to try to discredit me with the university. Seems to me hurting Asher means hurting Flood. So, I'm in. Also . . ."

I didn't know how to give voice to what I was feeling. It was Mal. His fight felt like my fight. Like I belonged at his side. I put a hand up. I meant to lay it on his chest but my fingers fluttered in midair a few inches from his skin. If I touched him again, I didn't know if I could stop. The pull between us was that strong.

I closed my fist and brought my hand down to my side. "What's happening to me? To us?"

Mal's face turned hard. I saw something pass through his eyes as if he warred with himself. Finally, he reached down and took my wrists in his hands. His fingers burned hot against my flesh. My heart raced in time with his as I watched a pulse beat in his temple.

"No," he said simply, but the force of the word seemed to strike me in the center of my chest, making my heart ache. "This isn't your fight. Get your things. I'm getting you the hell away from me."

Then, he let go of my wrists and my heart dropped to the floor.

Chapter Twelve

PART of me wanted to gather my dignity and storm out of the cabin on my own. I had tried to make my way to the Jeep once; I could do it again. This time, if Mal followed, I would find my resolve and keep on going. But, everything I told him in the cabin was true. I wanted to bring Flood down. If severing his connection with Asher's pack would help accomplish that goal, count me in. But, I couldn't deny the real reason my temper heated my blood. I just flat out didn't want to leave Mal. I didn't fully understand it, but being with him seemed natural. Like it was what I was meant to do.

For now though, I had to focus on the matter at hand. Getting to the ranger station, calling my department head, and filing a complaint against Byron Flood. It meant my internship was probably kaput for the time being, but I had to have faith the university would make things right. I was the aggrieved party, after all.

I busied myself finding the lost remnants of my clothing and stuffing them back in my pack. Mal waited by the door, twirling the car keys in his hand. I slung the shotgun back over my shoulder and gave him a nod when I was ready.

"I'll drive back myself," I said. "It's daylight. I think I can find my way to the ranger station."

"Are you sure?"

I nodded. "Completely. Just walk me back to the Jeep and I'll be on my way." I gave Mal a smug smile, not wanting to give him the satisfaction of seeing how much the idea of leaving him unsettled me. Mal gave me a quick nod and started walking toward me. He put a hand out, offering to take the backpack, but I waved him off. I carried the thing in here. I could carry it out.

He shrugged then pointed northeast. "About a hundred yards that way, you'll see a dense trail."

"Wait, you're not going with me?"

Mal smiled. "Oh, I'm gonna be close by, but I can keep a better lookout if I shift."

"Oh. Right. You uh, want me to wait for you while you do that?"

Mal pulled on the button of his jeans. I bit my lip and looked the other way. Silly, I know, but it was pretty tough to concentrate on being indignant with that body just a few feet away from me. Mal turned his back and I couldn't help it. I looked. He shifted so seamlessly, crouching low; the muscles of his back twisted, his shoulder blades rolled, and midnight black fur sprouted everywhere. Then, the black wolf trotted around me, his snout high in the air.

I gave him a nod, readjusted the weight of my backpack, and set off on the trail to the Jeep. Mal's wolf sprang in front of me, his powerful back legs propelling him. Then, he darted off into the thick of the trees to guard the way. With each step I took, I could feel him all around me, watching, guarding. We were connected by some invisible string, it seemed. It felt familiar, comforting. And now, he was asking me to sever it.

I wondered if that was the last I would see of him. My gut clenched at the thought of it. Could I really just get into the Jeep, drive off, and go back to my life as if everything were normal again? Like this was just some lost, wild weekend. No. The idea made me feel physically ill. I could never un-know what I knew about Mal and the others. There had to be a reason he made me feel the way he did. He was drawn to me just as much as I was drawn to him.

Well, I wasn't leaving Manistee right away. Not until I had everything settled with G.L.U. And I sure as hell wasn't heading back to California with nothing to show for the hard work I'd done here. It's probably exactly what Flood wanted. It's what he threatened back at the outpost just before Mal nearly ripped his throat out.

With each step I took rage at Flood and heartache at leaving Mal turned into resolve. I wasn't giving any of this up without a fight. Not my future. Not my scholarship. And not what I shared with Mal. One way or another we weren't finished. As the thick brush gave way to a trail, I listened for Mal. I could sense him nearby, darting through the trees, making sure we were alone. But, he didn't show himself again. After about twenty minutes, I saw the Jeep up ahead, partially obscured by the branches Mal had thrown over it.

My heart quickened. The Jeep represented a return to a somewhat normal part of my life before the last twenty-four hours upended everything. I went to the back and lifted the hatch. I threw my pack on the floor and slid the shotgun off my shoulder, carefully tucking it in beside the pack. I reached up and slammed the hatch shut. A pair of golden eyes flashed through the brush. Mal.

I wanted him to shift again, wanted to watch the cruel beauty of it. I wanted to kiss him goodbye. He blinked once then receded further into the woods. I let out the breath I'd been holding and twirled the keys on my index finger.

The sun was high above me. It had to be close to noon. I slid into the driver's seat and saw the corner of my cell phone peeking out from a corner of the floor mat on the passenger's side. Reaching over to pick it up, the screen was black. The battery had run out probably hours ago. Something I'd have to worry about later. For now, I needed to get to the ranger station and work on putting the pieces of my life back together.

I put the car in gear and drove through the thick trail, crunching twigs and branches beneath the tires. I kept checking the mirrors, hoping I might catch a last glimpse of Mal. I sensed him back there still, but he stayed hidden. After a few minutes, the trail turned to gravel, and I knew I was heading the right way.

My pulse raced as I pulled into the ranger station. Two patrol cars were parked out front. It occurred to me I hadn't given a single thought about what the hell I was going to tell them. Certainly nothing about Mal. If they believed me at all, I couldn't risk the chance that they were allied with Asher's pack and might want to do him harm like Flood did.

I put the car in park, slid the keys in my back pocket, and headed for the front door. The place was empty when I went inside. The station served as a tourist information and nature center for the whole park as well. Photographs lined the wall laying out the park's timeline dating back to the nineteenth century. Large stuffed bears, badgers, deer and other wildlife were posed next to information kiosks all throughout the room, each of them staring silently back at me with glassy black eyes. But, other than that, the place seemed empty. I walked further in past the gift shop. Beyond it, a long hallway led to the command center -- such as it was -- for the ranger station.

I heard a squawking police radio and low voices. Classified ads, sheriff's auction notices, and wanted posters festooned a corkboard on the wall. I took a breath to call out for one of the rangers, but something caught my eye. If it hadn't, if I *had* called out, I shudder to think what might have happened instead of what did.

Most of the rest of the papers on that corkboard were crinkled or tattered from weeks or months of hanging there. But, one at the center was fresh and crisp, and the colored picture at the center still shone. I swallowed the words I meant to shout and turned to see my own face staring back at me. A bad copy of the picture from my student I.D. smiled timidly back at me under large black lettering, "Person of Interest."

My heart flipped in my chest. I chanced a look back down the hall as I unpinned the wanted poster and quietly stepped back toward the nature center. My fingers shook as I skimmed the copy on the poster. Only phrases leaped out at me, I didn't seem able to focus long enough to read full sentences.

Wanted for questioning in the assault on Byron Flood.

Grand Theft Auto

Considered armed and extremely dangerous

The words jumbled around in my brain, free floating while I tried to process what I was seeing. Make sense of it. Me. Wanted for questioning. They thought I assaulted Flood? Deep laughter came from down the hall, growing closer. I pressed myself against the wall, hiding behind a large stuffed brown bear.

Should I talk to the rangers? Turn myself in? This was all just a horrible misunderstanding. But, on some preternatural level, I sensed extreme danger. This was Flood's doing. Of course it was. His last venomous words to me rang through my brain.

You're finished. At the college. Everywhere. You think I'm going to let some little cocktease slut like you get away with this? You'll be lucky if expulsion is the worst thing that happens to you. This is my *park. My people.*

Oh my God. His people. His park. If he'd been telling the truth, the rangers on the other end of that hallway might not believe anything I had to say. Before I even knew what I was doing, I found myself backing out of the room toward the door. I crumpled the wanted poster in my fist and shoved it in my back pocket. I turned and stumbled out the door. Air stabbed into my lungs as my pulse raced.

Where could I go? Who could I trust? Help. I needed help. A lawyer. Someone. I reached into my other pocket and pulled out the keys.

The keys to the Jeep. Words from the poster finally penetrated my brain. The Jeep. Flood told them I'd stolen it. That meant the cops were looking for it as much as me. And there it was, parked in the first open space at the front of the ranger station. I ran to the back of it, scanning the parking lot and the woods behind it. For now, no one seemed to be watching. I pulled my backpack out of the back and slung it over my shoulder. I meant to quietly close the hatch but something stopped me. Without even thinking, I grabbed the shotgun and closed the door.

Where could I go? The instant I thought it, the answer was

clear. Rational or not, I trusted exactly one person in this entire state right now. Mal. I could go back to Mal. The decision seemed to move through me, making my heart slow down to normal and my head fully clear.

I looked back one more time at the station to make sure no one saw me leave, then I headed back into the forest and ran.

Chapter Thirteen

I DON'T THINK I had a conscious thought about what direction to go. It was like my feet seemed to know where to carry me. I couldn't sense Mal like I had when I left the cabin, and yet he seemed to call to me, like a beacon. Faint, but still powerful. I just hoped he'd be willing to help me when I did find him. And I hoped I could make it there before one of Asher's pack found me first.

I don't know how long I ran. Long enough that my legs started to feel numb. Long enough that my throat went dry as sandpaper. Each breath I took stabbed through my lungs as my heart kept racing.

But no one seemed to give chase. If the rangers noticed the Jeep parked in their lot, they hadn't charged after me in the woods. Absurd. Insane. How could anyone think that I was guilty of the things Flood told them about me? Cam knew the truth. Had every single moment of what I thought was friendship been a lie? Sure, he'd brought me back to the camp when I wanted to go, but he knew the truth, didn't he? Did he hate me so much he'd let Flood ruin me like this? The moment I thought it, the answer settled in my gut, forming a cold pit. Of course Cam hadn't stood up for me. He covered his own ass and his own future. His future was directly tied to Flood's. Well, mine wasn't. Not anymore.

It was hard to think of anything more than the few minutes, few seconds ahead of me. I had no allies in the world except maybe the only one that mattered. I just hoped I could make it to Mal before it was too late. What if he hadn't gone back to the cabin? I pushed back the icy fingers of panic threatening to weigh me down. I'd gotten this far. Whatever happened, I'd find a way to deal. With each step I took I went deeper into the thick woods. I left the ranger station and everything familiar far behind. In some ways, it seemed like I'd been surrounded by these woods forever. My old life was gone. What lay in front of me, no matter what, would never be the same.

I got careless as all these thoughts swirled in my brain. I took a wrong step and thick branches entangled my ankle. I went down hard, landing on my right hip.

"Shit." I grimaced. I set the shotgun beside me and freed my leg. Shooting pain went down my leg, but I knew I hadn't broken anything. I took a breath and looked around. I'd reached the densest part of the forest, far from any of the ranger's trails. Sweat poured down the back of my neck. Leaves and twigs stuck to my clothes and tangled my hair. God, I had to look like I belonged here now. Some wild thing thrashing on the forest floor.

I got my feet under me and leaned down to grab my pack. A twig cracked to my left, loud as a firecracker. I crouched low and grabbed the gun, tucking it carefully under my right arm. At first, I couldn't see anything. Then, a flock of birds took flight all at once from the branches of a large elm in front of me, shaking the leaves as they went.

Something was moving toward me. Something big.

I whirled around, sliding my left hand down the barrel of the shotgun, I racked a round and jammed the stock into my right shoulder. My fingers closed around the trigger as I looked through the scope. But, the lens was fogged. I couldn't see a damn thing.

A blur of motion came toward me. Gray fur. Cold eyes. White fangs glinting in the sunlight. Then the wolf stopped running. He crouched low, held his tail high and snarled as he approached.

Two seconds. Two breaths. Fire flashed in the wolf's eyes as he lunged. I squeezed the trigger. The recoil knocked me backward, flat on my ass, but I kept my grip on the gun. The wolf howled once as it happened and I saw a cloud of red burst from his right shoulder. Adrenalin propelled the wolf forward. Though my own shoulder screamed in pain from the impact, I raised the gun again and racked another round, ready to take the kill shot.

The wolf dropped just a few feet in front of me and skidded, his teeth still bared, his nostrils flared from the effort of breathing. But, he was no longer a threat.

I sank to my knees, stumbling forward. I laid the gun on the ground and knelt in front of him. Dark blood poured out of the gaping wound on his shoulder. I'd aimed too far to the left. I could see the shell had not penetrated but actually grazed him, tearing a gash the size of a baseball across his shoulder and part of his right flank. Had my shot gone just a few inches to the right, I likely would have blown his head clean off.

Still, as blood leached out of the massive wound, the wolf fixed his gaze on mine. He didn't shift, but his eyes dimmed, becoming more human than wolf as his life started to drain away. There was so much blood. It coated the wolf's fur, turning him more brown than gray. It matted the leaves in front of him.

I wanted to touch him. I can't explain it. Like everything that had happened to me since the moment Mal stepped into my life, my instincts turned inside out. This wolf was a killer. If I hadn't gotten the shot off, he would have torn me to bits. I'd seen the bloodlust clouding his cold green eyes.

But all that was gone now. All that remained was a creature in pain. And yet, I knew he wasn't alone. He had a pack nearby and my gunshot had echoed through the trees. Black crows already circled overhead as the smell of death reached their senses.

I gave one last look to the dying wolf and found my feet beneath me. The trauma of the last few moments disoriented me. I couldn't remember what direction I'd been headed. I closed my eyes and tried to slow my wildly beating heart. I had a strange compulsion to call out to Mal, even though I knew it was foolish. Drawing even more attention to my position could prove deadly.

I took the first halting steps forward, trusting my instincts to lead the way. The wolf let out pitiful whine behind me. I felt pulled to him too, but staying here would only bring danger. There was nothing else I could do for the creature. And after all, if he weren't the one lying there dying, I would be.

I took another step then froze. Wind rustled through the trees and I saw another flash of fur in the distance. This time, I didn't have enough time to aim the shotgun.

My heart sank to my knees as the black wolf leaped toward me, skidding to a halt just a few inches from me. My legs turned to jelly and I found myself kneeling before Mal. His eyes blazed wild as I reached for him. Before I could touch him, his fur shifted and rolled. With frightening speed, the black wolf became the man. Mal towered over me, his sculpted from dripping with sweat.

"Laura," his voice sounded more animal than human. "Are you all right?"

I nodded. I couldn't form my own words yet. I gestured by turning my head back toward the dying wolf. Mal looked back at me, his eyes wide. He put a hand on my shoulder then passed me. He dropped to his knees before the injured wolf and tore a hand through his hair.

"Jesus. Laura. What have you done?"

His words penetrated my brain and cleared the fog. "I what? Mal, he would have ripped me apart."

Mal nodded as he cradled the wolf's head in his hands. "I know. Fuck. I know."

I readjusted the shotgun strap on my shoulder and went to him. "Is that him? Did I kill Asher?"

Mal shut his eyes tight and swallowed hard, shaking his head. "I wish to God you had. No. This isn't Asher. This is Luke."

Mal looked up toward the sky. His shoulders quaked with an emotion I couldn't place. Rage? Grief? Fear? Maybe all three. He threw his head back and yelled, "Fuck!"

I knelt beside him. "What was I supposed to do?"

Mal didn't seem to see me for a moment. He smoothed a hand over Luke's ears. The light had gone out of the wolf's eyes. Blood still poured from the wound on his shoulder so I didn't think he was dead. Yet.

"Help me," Mal finally said. "Do you have something in your bag? Something we can press into the wound and try to stop the bleeding?"

"What?"

"Laura!" Mal's tone was harsh, commanding. It sent a shiver through me.

"Mal, why? Didn't I tell you this one tried to kill me? Just like you said."

Mal's eyes flashed as he focused them on me. "And now, you're going to help me save his life. But, we have to hurry. Asher and the others will be here any minute."

"Wha-what are we going to do?"

"We're going to get the hell out of here as fast as we can. And we're going to take him with us."

Chapter Fourteen

I GRABBED a shirt and a towel out of my pack and tossed them to Mal. He pressed the shirt into Luke's wound, then wrapped the towel around his shoulder as best he could.

"We've got to hurry," Mal said. "Luke? Can you hear me? Don't try to shift."

The injured wolf's head lolled to the side I saw the faint rise and fall of his chest. His breathing was slow and shallow.

"Can you run?" Mal said to me.

I nodded.

"Good. I can't shift. I don't think you're strong enough to carry him. How good are you with that thing?" He gestured with his chin toward the shotgun.

I cocked my head to the side as he hoisted Luke over his shoulder. The wolf's great head hung limp down to the middle of Mal's back. I gestured above my own left eyebrow and pointed to his. "I'd say I'm a hell of a lot better with this thing than Byron Flood was. If I weren't I'd be dead right now."

Mal clenched his jaw and gave me a quick nod. "Good. Stay sharp. Step exactly where I step. You see anything on four legs bigger than a squirrel headed our way, shoot it."

I didn't have a chance to answer him. Mal started running northwest. Fast. I heaved my backpack to my other shoulder and took off after him, trying to do as he said. Even on two legs and lugging one hundred and forty-odd pounds of almost dead wolf over his shoulder, Mal was unbelievably fast. I couldn't hope to keep up, so I just tried to keep him within my line of sight.

Every movement, every sound around us sent my pulse spiking. In the distance, I heard a haunting howl and my blood ran cold. Mal didn't stop. He pushed through the dense forest, using his free arm as a battering ram against any branches or foliage that might impede me. When we came to a swift running stream he stopped.

I gasped for air; my lungs felt like they might explode. Mal barely looked winded.

"We cross here," he said. "Get wet. Up to your hips at least if you can. The stream's swollen now, so that shouldn't be a problem. We'll stay in the water for a hundred yards or so and work our way upstream. That ought to be enough to throw anyone following off the scent for now."

Then, Mal plunged into the stream. I followed. The water was deeper than I realized, coming to my chest. I held the shotgun above my head, but my pack got drenched. I had the fleeting thought that my cell phone was probably bricked for good now, but knew it might never matter again. The cold stabbed through me like a thousand tiny knives, but I kept up with Mal. For a brief moment, Luke opened his eyes. They fixed on me, then clouded over again as Mal dragged him through the water, washing away a good deal of the caked blood. I hoped that would help throw anyone off the scent too.

We made our way upstream then crawled up an embankment. Mal reached back to help me up the steepest part of it. His skin burned hot where mine was like ice. I longed to have him wrap me in his warmth as my teeth chattered loudly.

"We're almost there," Mal said. "About half a mile more. We'll make it."

Nodding, I hauled myself up the final steps and fell in behind him. Mal took off running again. My thighs burned, but I managed to keep up.

Finally, I saw Mal's rustic cabin through the trees. It looked like heaven. I knew we still faced danger out here exposed like this, but my body had been pushed to its limit. If I didn't get to stop soon, my legs would give out.

Mal got to the front door and kicked it open with his foot. I followed close behind and latched the door after me. Mal gently laid Luke down on the braided rug in front of the fireplace. I leaned the shotgun against the wall, set my soaked pack down, brought the two propane lanterns close, and lit them.

"Keep pressure on this," Mal said, pressing the soaked shirt into Luke's wound.

I knelt beside him. Hesitating at first, I took the shirt from Mal and pressed both of my hands down hard, trying to staunch the blood flow. I could already see it had stopped considerably, but a slow, constant, deadly trickle oozed through the cloth.

"This won't be enough," I said. "He's lost too much blood. If you want him to live, he needs a doctor. Or a vet."

Mal rummaged under the bed and pulled out the first aid kit.

He tore the top off the bottle of iodine and knelt beside me. I pulled back the cloth, hissing through my teeth. The wound was ugly, jagged. I could see bits of Luke's shoulder bone. I had to have hit some major blood vessels.

Mal poured half the bottle of iodine into the wound and unwound a thick wad of gauze. He pressed it against the wound and held it tight. Then, he shifted into a seated position and leaned his head against the stone hearth, resting Luke's head in his lap.

"What do we do now?"

Mal let out a breath. "Just this. More of this."

"Mal. I told you, he's lost too much blood. I don't know what a werewolf's heart rate is supposed to be, but his is weak. Erratic." I pressed a hand against the beast's neck, feeling for a pulse. It was faint and thready, just like I'd described.

"He's not going to die," Mal said. "Not if we can get the bleeding to stop and keep the wound from getting infected. He'll heal. We're harder to kill than that. Next time, if you ever have to, make sure you hit the head or the heart."

I opened my mouth to protest or ask a thousand other questions. But, seeing the look in Mal's eyes, I clamped my jaw shut. He would heal. Of course he would. Luke wasn't fully human or fully wolf. I'd seen Mal's inhuman strength and speed with my own eyes. If any being could survive a wound like that with just a glorified bandage, a werewolf certainly could. I couldn't decide whether I was rooting for this one's recovery or demise just at the moment.

Nodding, I shifted my weight so I sat on the floor directly in front of Mal. I took the roll of gauze from him and started tearing off fresh strips, lining them side by side on the ledge of the stone hearth beside us.

"What can I do?" I asked.

Mal looked at me. His eyes glinted in the warm, amber light cast by the lanterns. It was still early afternoon, but clouds had rolled in, blocking the sunlight. A storm brewed to the northeast. I heard the first echoes of rolling thunder.

"That's good for us," he said. "It'll make it that much harder for Asher and the rest of the pack to figure out where we went."

I nodded and drew my knees to my chest, shivering in my wet clothes. I wished we could light the fireplace but knew that would draw way too much attention.

"I'll get you home," Mal said. "I promise."

I held up a hand. I don't know why, but I didn't want to hear him promise me anything. Not then. Home would be the first place law enforcement would look for me. Heat stabbed through me. In all of this, I hadn't thought about my family. By now, they had to have heard Flood's version of what happened. God. I wished I could call them. Explain.

"What were you doing out there?" Mal said after a long silence. "Why didn't you do what I told you?"

There was no accusation in his voice, but he seemed defeated, fully of worry. Deep lines furrowed his brow. I had the urge to go to him again, touch the tender spot where Flood's shot had ricocheted off the tree the other day and marred his flesh. But, something had shifted between us. The last hour, as we ran for our lives together, a bond had formed to join the one we made when I let him take me on the forest floor.

"I tried," I finally said. I mulled the words I wanted to say to find a way to explain. Then, I remembered the wanted poster. I leaned forward and pulled it carefully out of my back pocket. It was soggy, the edges tattered, but the text and picture were still legible. I handed it to Mal. He reached over and took it. That now familiar spark flared through me when his fingers touched mine. Exhausted as I was, physically and emotionally spent, the urge to go to him, to let him touch me and claim me still burned strong.

Mal's eyes darted over the fragile paper. He banged his head gently against the stone hearth and let out a sigh. "Son of a bitch."

"Yep. Apparently, I'm a bit of an outlaw too now."

"Laura, I'm sorry."

"Why? This part wasn't you. I know what you did for me, Mal. I know if you hadn't come when you did, Flood would have raped me or worse."

Mal flinched when I said it. His eyes flashed gold, going from man to wolf then back again. He let out a low growl and curled his fist at his side. Then, he pressed his eyes shut tight and got a hold of himself.

"I'll kill him," he said, and I knew instantly it wasn't an empty threat.

"I hope it won't come to that. I need him to confess and tell the cops the truth. Unless Cam grows a pair and does the right thing, it's my word against his for the moment."

"And mine," Mal said, his voice dark with menace.

"Right. And you're in a position to march up to the ranger station and give a statement now? In case you hadn't noticed, we're in a bit of a pickle. We've got a pack of killer wolves on our tail who are more than likely in cahoots with Byron Flood *and* the ranger service. We try to go back there now, and I'm thinking that's walking into a trap. Plus, what about him? If we leave Luke now, he'll bleed out on your floor. I'm trying to figure out why that's supposed to bother me. Except I know it bothers you. And why exactly do your moods seem to affect mine now?"

Mal smiled.

"Why are we doing this?" I asked. Now that it looked like we had at least a little time to ourselves, I wanted solid answers. "Why are we going through all this trouble to keep him alive? I thought your objective was to defeat Asher."

"Asher. Not the rest of the pack. Luke is . . . a friend."

"He sure as hell didn't act like it."

Mal smoothed his hand over Luke's ear. He was unconscious, but his breathing had eased.

"He can't control his actions. Asher does."

"God. Is that what it means to live as a werewolf? You have to do your Alpha's bidding even if you don't like it?"

Mal looked at some unseen point over my shoulder. "No. It's not always like that. Alphas have the power to control a pack, but it's something that should only be used rarely. Only if there's no other choice. What Asher's doing is a perversion of everything we are. And a good Alpha doesn't *have* to control members of a pack against their will. You're supposed to *want* to follow."

"And you're saying you're sure Luke doesn't?"

"Luke has deeper roots in Wild Lake than anyone. But he's

been gone and under Asher's influence for a very long time. Still, I don't think he'd choose this path if Asher wasn't forcing it on him. God, it's complicated."

"Why?"

"Because Asher is his brother. Well, half-brother. They have different mothers."

"Hmm. Once again, that seems pretty simple. So Luke left Wild Lake and went with Asher out of family loyalty. But, it turns out Asher is a psychopathic maniac who's just out for revenge against anyone from Wild Lake. Only now, Luke's stuck because Asher can pretty much make him do anything he wants him to whether he likes it or not."

Mal laughed. "Okay. Yeah. I guess maybe not as complicated as I thought."

"So, what you have to figure out is a way to kill Asher without either hurting the rest of the pack or getting killed yourself."

"Right."

"Okay. And now you've got a bargaining chip because you've got Asher's brother. Assuming he doesn't die. And now *I'm* in deep shit because I just *shot* Asher's brother so now he's got an extra special reason to hate my ass other than the fact I'm kind of on your side."

"Also right."

"Got it. So what's to stop Luke from trying to rip my or your guts out again as soon as he wakes up and starts feeling frisky again?"

"Well, I'm planning to tie him up."

"Okay."

"Tight."

"Good plan. But how does Asher control him? I mean, is it mind control?"

"In a way, yes. It's a compulsion. An urge you can't suppress. In an emergency, it can save your life because the pack works as a unit. But Asher is using his pack as his own personal army of vengeance. He brought them to your outpost because of me."

I folded my arms in front of me and cocked my head to the side. "And you were there because of me?"

Mal brushed his hand across his thigh, flaking off some of the dried mud that still clung to his jeans. "Yes."

Butterflies took roost behind my ribcage. Mal had come for me. I knew it mattered. There was something bigger going on between us besides lust. But, he didn't tell me any more. Not just then. I wasn't sure I was ready to hear it. It was enough that I *felt* it. Craving. That's as close as I can come to explaining the emotion roiling inside me. My body, my *soul* was starting to need Mal near me on some elemental level. It excited me, made my heart race, and terrified me. I let out a breath and pivoted the conversation. As much as I wanted to explore what was happening between us, there was still a very real threat looming in the dark woods.

"So can Asher tell where Luke is right now? Could he lead Asher straight to us without even meaning to?"

"Normally, yes. That's a risk. But Luke's unconscious and he's lost a lot of blood. His heart even stopped beating a few times as I was carrying him out. He's not transmitting anything right now, and I covered our scent when we came out. Mother Nature is about to cover our tracks the rest of the way as soon as that storm blows in about twenty minutes. It's a temporary fix, but we're safe for now."

I nodded. I hugged my knees to my chest. My teeth rattled together as I shivered. Mal carefully shifted Luke's head to the floor and came to me. He wrapped his arms and his body heat around me. I let out a sigh as I leaned against him, pressing my cheek against the hard outlines of his chest.

As he pulled me in close, I felt like I belonged there. Like everything in my life would forever be defined as before I met Mal and after. My world was turned upside down. Everything I knew and had worked for had slipped away beneath my feet. I should be panicked, devastated. But, as Mal held me like that, I just felt peaceful. Protected.

I could hear Mal's heart beating steady and strong beneath my ear. It took me a moment to recognize it, but my own heart had slowed and now matched his. This man exerted some kind of biofeedback over me that had me filled with both fear and wonderment. He'd answered most of my questions about Asher and Luke; I needed to know more about what was happening to me. To us. Ready or not, I had to know the truth. I shifted so I sat between Mal's legs and lifted my head off his chest, tilting my head to look up at him.

"Did you do something to me?" I asked.

Mal reached out and traced a line above my brow with his thumb then smoothed my hair back. His eyes were warm, but his face grew dark as he swallowed hard.

"I couldn't help it."

"Couldn't help what?"

"Do you feel drawn to me?"

My turn to swallow past a lump in my throat as I considered my answer. "Yes. It's different than anything I've ever experienced. I seem to, I don't know, feel you. I like it better when you're touching me a whole lot more than when you're not. It's lust, but that's not all of it, is it?"

Mal shook his head. "No." He dropped his hand from my face and stared up at the ceiling, biting his lip as he smiled. Then, he turned his head back toward me and fixed those glinting eyes on me, making my blood simmer.

"I didn't go looking for it. I was mated once, to another woman. I thought we were fated. She chose another Alpha. It's part of the reason I was sent away. Then, as soon as I got some distance from it, from *her*, I knew it wasn't what I thought. But, then I saw you in the woods that day. It was . . . different."

"I belong to you." In my head, I meant it as a question. But, by the time my lips formed the words, I knew the truth of them in my heart. Possessiveness, tinged with a fair bit of anger broiled inside me at even the mention of Mal with another woman. God, even though I knew I had no right. I'd known him for all of a few days. And yet, it wasn't just the feeling that I belonged to him. He belonged to *me*, dammit.

His eyes locked with mine, blazing bright. He worked the strong muscles of his jaw as he brought his hand up again and cradled my cheek with his.

"You're supposed to be mine."

"What does that mean?" The air in the room seemed to thicken. As Mal's fingers trailed from my cheek around to the nape of my neck, it got harder to breathe. Every nerve ending seemed attuned to his. I felt his heat, his light, and a more urgent need down below as his cock stiffened against my thigh as I sat with my legs draped across his lap.

"I may not have a pack of my own yet, but I'm an Alpha, Laura."

I blinked hard, trying to process his words. He was an Alpha. Just like Asher. If I let him, would he have the power to control me the way Asher controlled Luke? The thought of it made me shudder. At the same time, a dark hunger rose inside me. Desire heated my blood, making my sex throb. I wanted it. I wanted Mal. Some primal urge flooded through me at the idea of letting Mal take control.

"Asher will keep coming. He'll use any means to try and bring me down. And it's not just me. If I fail, he'll keep coming after the Wild Lake packs. I've put you at risk because now he knows you're connected to me. But, you're not as connected as you can be."

My pulse thundered in my ears, which meant Mal's did too. My breath hitched. I knew it. It was like I understood what he was going to say before he said it. A question. An ultimatum. My body knew the answer. I struggled to think with my head.

"If I mark you as mine . . . for real, I can protect you, Laura. And if something happens to me, you can go to Wild Lake and they'll protect you. They may have banished me, but they can't turn you away."

Something tore inside me at the thought of anything happening to Mal. God. I couldn't breathe.

"But it also means there can be no question you belong to me. It'll make you an even bigger prize to Asher and any enemy of the Wild Lake packs."

I nodded. Again, my mind reeled trying to process what he was saying even though my body already seemed to understand. I moved toward him, hesitating for just a fraction of a second, knowing intuitively I'd reached the point of no return.

Then we moved beyond words. Mal gently gripped my arms and pulled me close, pressing his lips to mine. He kissed me lightly at first. I sensed him struggle to keep his own dark desires at bay, unsure of whether I could face them. But, I could. God help me, I knew I could.

Before I gave it conscious thought, I found myself tearing at my shirt, forcing it over my head. My breasts sprang free as I rose up and straddled Mal's thighs. He looked up at me, running his hands along my ribcage. My skin raised in gooseflesh as he rolled his thumbs across my sensitive nipples, making them rise to peaks.

"Mal," I gasped. I flung my arms around his neck and wrapped my legs around his hips as he stood up, lifting me easily as if I weighed nothing. I got dizzy as he whirled us around and headed for the door. Unlatching it, he carried me outside.

The rain had just started to fall. A moment ago, I had shivered from the cold. Now, with my body wrapped around Mal's, his heat engulfed me. I tilted my head, letting raindrops fall across my forehead, dampening my hair. With four quick strides, Mal had me pressed against a thick maple. I dropped my legs and threaded my fingers through the thick hair at the nape of his neck.

"Do you want this?" he said, his voice ragged with lust.

"Yes." I choked the word out, not really wanting to speak, but only wanting to feel. I closed my eyes and tilted my head back, waiting to feel his mouth on mine.

But Mal tilted my head down with his thumb against my chin.

"Open your eyes," he whispered. When I did, his eyes flashed from the black wolf's to his own again. Heat rushed through me, settling between my legs. While the driving rain soaked my skin, warmth spread through me, making my most sensitive flesh throb for him.

"You're mine. Do you understand? Do you want this?"

My eyes snapped open wide. I couldn't help that desire made the corners of my mouth lift in a slow, sultry smile. Oh, yes. I wanted this.

"Laura," he said again, his tone more urgent. "I mean to claim you. For good. Do you understand? It has to be what you want."

So, he would give me a choice. As desire raced through me, I knew he wanted my eyes open and my mind clear. I didn't fully understand what he meant, not then. I only knew that when he said it, every cell in my body cried out, "Yes! Oh, God, yes!"

"Say it," he said through gritted teeth. His hands went to his belt, ripping open the buckle and sliding the thin leather strap through the loops. My eyes went to it, the corded veins in his strong hands and the smell of wet leather. Desire flashed through me as I thought about what it would feel like if he used it on me. The zinging sound it made when he whipped it through the last belt buckle and dropped it to the ground made a fresh gush of juices pool between my legs. I was so ready for him. Slowly, I unfastened the button of my own jeans and tried to wriggle out of them. Thoroughly soaked from the rain, they clung to me like a second skin, trapping my legs inside.

"Say it, Laura," he said, his voice sexy and low. "I have to hear it."

"Yes," I whispered, my voice trembling. "I want you to."

"What?"

"Claim me. Yes. Please. Make me yours."

He stepped out of his jeans and cast them aside. Then he hooked his fingers through my belt loops and jerked me toward him. I gasped as he dragged my jeans and panties down, giving me enough space to kick out of them. He took a step back and looked at me. I stood with my hands behind me, one leg crooked against the trunk of the tree. My breasts quivered as my breath came hot and heavy. Droplets of rain clung to his dark hair, pasting it against his forehead.

"Good," he said, his voice barely more than a growl. Heat pulsed between my thighs. I was soaked for him. Swollen. Ready. He reached out and slid a gentle finger across my clit. His fingers were so hot. I shuddered at his touch, as he discovered just how eager I was. "So good, baby." He sucked air through his teeth.

"Please, Mal. Don't make me wait."

Thunder cracked all around us. The wind rose, making the tree tops sway. Mal's shoulders quaked with his seductive laugh. "Get on your hands and knees, Laura."

I didn't hesitate. I dropped down to all fours, stretching myself out on the bed of soft, wet wild grass. He didn't have to tell me. I spread my legs wide. He leaned down and put a gentle hand at the small of my back, pressing me down a little further so my ass thrust up even higher for him. I gasped as heat flared through me, making my swollen clit ache and throb for him even more.

"That's it, baby. Now brace yourself," he whispered. "This time, I can't be gentle."

Chapter Fifteen

MAL SLID two fingers across my swollen sex, opening me wider for him. I dug my fingers into the soft earth. My body shuttered as he pressed the head of his cock against my slick opening. He worked me, tugging gently on my sensitive bud, making me tremble with desire and expectation. God, I was so primed already. All that I was seemed centered around that sensitive space between my legs. But, Mal took his time, working me into a lather to where I couldn't think about anything but him. Rough. Hot. Wild.

My body seemed to know what to do. I arched my back, bringing my hips higher, stretching my inner thighs as wide as they could go. My legs started to shake as I held myself in position. But, everything in me told me this is what he needed. Me, stretched out on all fours, leaving myself exposed to him completely. I was his for the taking, and this is how I needed to prove it. I begged for him with my body and my words.

"Yes. Please. Oh, God, Mal. Do it!"

Finally . . . mercifully, he withdrew his fingers and put his hands firmly on my hips angling me back even further so I had to struggle to keep my knees in position. He took a breath and in that split second before he entered me, I knew everything about me would shift yet again. I welcomed it. Craved it. Craved him.

He thrust himself deep, stretching me wide. I cried out from the pleasure of it and tried to keep my legs from buckling beneath him. He was huge and hard and I took in the full length of him. He thrust deep and strong. I gripped the ground tight to keep myself still. He reached around again and his fingers found my clit. He stroked me as he pumped me deep.

I found my voice again. "Yes," I cried. "God. Yes! Please!"

My body knew what it craved even if my mind had no concept. This was different than the day before. I understood it now. As mind-blowing as that had been, Mal had held back somehow. But this. This. He filled every corner of me. Body and soul. I felt part of him. He was part of me. The more he gave me, the more I wanted. All of it. All of him. I couldn't bear not having him touch me. Not having him fuck me. How had I lived twenty years without this?

His body vibrated in a low growl. I knew he warred with the beast inside of him. I wanted to face him, watch the brilliant flash of gold as I sated the man and quelled the beast.

I felt his balls seize against me and knew he was close. I struggled to open myself ever wider to take him all in. Part of me didn't want him to come yet. I wanted to savor this because I knew instinctively this would change us both forever. I felt the surge within him and knew he couldn't hold back much longer. With skillful fingers, Mal worked me, bringing me to my own cresting desire. I couldn't contain it. Not for another second. Stars flashed in front of my eyes as my knees started to shake.

My orgasm began to rip through me, spreading from the core of my being to the roots of my hair to the tips of my toes. Still though, I knew something was missing. I still felt like I had more of myself to give. A different burning need rose within me. One I couldn't understand.

But, Mal did.

His thrusts became erratic as he struggled to contain his own desire. Then, he went rigid behind me. He pressed one hand flat on my back then ran it up, threading his fingers through my hair. He moved my hair aside and leaned forward until I could feel his breath against my ear.

Just that small shift in his posture as he leaned down bringing his head close to mine sent heat zinging through me. He was in me now as deep as he could go. My walls clenched around him as I shuddered through the last of my orgasm. Yes. This. All of him. All of me. I never wanted it to stop.

"Are you ready?" he whispered.

"Y-yes."

He leaned down even further, flicking his tongue along the base of my neck. That powerful need rose in me again and I knew I was about to have a second explosive orgasm on the tail of the first. That had never happened to me before. On instinct, I knew that was just the first of many new things opening myself to this man would bring.

An instant later, he proved me right. As the second, even more powerful orgasm coursed through me, Mal pressed his lips against my skin and bared his teeth. I felt a sharp stab of pain at the base of my neck, followed immediately by a flood of warmth. He let out a low growl that vibrated through me, hitting every pleasure center and making me gasp. Heat spread through me, starting at that point on my neck and joining with the throbbing pleasure between my legs. My whole body shook from it. Then, Mal shot his seed deep inside me. I felt penetrated in every pore.

Something was happening. Mal wasn't just inside of me anymore. He was part of me. His pulse became my pulse. My heart beat for his. For an instant, I went outside of myself. Or rather, I went inside of *him*. I saw myself through Mal's eyes. My head thrown back, my back arched. Everything else around me drew sharply into focus. As if I could see infrared.

And the hunger.

In that flash of time, I felt it as Mal did. Burning desire unlike any I'd ever known. Fearsome. Primal. Mine. I was Mal and Mal was me. Stronger together than each of us ever had been apart.

I had two centers of desire. The one between my legs and something new. At the base of my neck, where Mal had marked me, heat pulsed there in perfect time with my heartbeat and now his.

It was as if nothing had ever happened to me except for this moment. It was all that I was. All that I needed. Just me. Just Mal. The woods, the scents and sounds, somehow, they were all part of us too. I cried out. My voice no longer sounding like my own, as if I were part beast now too. Thunder boomed and lightening cracked all around us, illuminating the woods in blue. I should be afraid. Seek shelter. But, Mal was all the shelter I needed. The storm seemed part of this too. Soaking us. Washing away whatever we were before this moment and leaving something new and stronger behind.

Chapter Sixteen

LATER, after Mal spent every last drop inside me, my legs finally gave way and I buckled beneath him. Mal put a firm hand on my ribcage and gently guided me to the ground beside him.

Panting. Spent. I curved my body around his and rested my head against his chest as he smoothed the hair away from my face and feathered soft kisses over the crown of my head.

I don't know how much time passed. Forever. A second. The pouring rain gave way to a light mist. We were both drenched from it and from each other. I should be cold. Freezing. Except I wasn't. I'd never felt more safe, warm, or protected in my life. Finally, when I could just start to feel my bones again, I lifted my head and looked at him. Mal tilted his head and smiled at me.

"What. Was. That?" My words were hard to form as I still gasped for air.

Mal's deep laughter vibrated through me. It seemed that's the way it would always be from now on. I felt what he felt. He warmed me.

"I've marked you, Princess. You're mine. And I guess I'm yours."

Maybe the news should have shocked me. But, like everything else about him, it felt natural. Right. He filled in missing pieces of myself I hadn't known were lost.

"What does it mean?"

"You know what it means. You can feel it."

And I could. My heart seemed to beat for Mal's quite literally now. He shifted, bringing himself up on one elbow; he leaned down and kissed me. "And it means that no matter where you are, I'll always be able to sense you. If you're frightened. If you're in pain I'll know it and I'll be able to find you. You belong to me, Laura. And I belong to you. We're fated mates. Do you understand?"

"I think so. God. Mal. It makes sense. I know that sounds crazy, but it does. I feel like I've been waiting for you my whole life and never realized it until now. How is that possible?"

He leaned down and kissed me. "That's just how it works. Sometimes, anyway. I'm just sorry about the timing."

"But, this isn't something you plan for, is it? I mean, it just happens when it happens right? How could *anyone* plan for it any more than you can plan for getting struck by lightning?"

Mal flashed a smile that sent heat through me again. God. My legs had turned to rubber. I was sore in muscles I never knew I had and probably wouldn't be able to walk straight for hours. And yet, I already wanted him again.

He reached over and gently tweaked my nipple, making it rise for him. He could make every part of me rise for him at any moment. Desire coursed through me as I knew how much I wanted him to. I loved the way he made me feel. I leaned up and kissed him.

"Well, now that you have me right where you want me, what do you plan to do to me?" I smiled up at him.

He rolled to his back and threaded his fingers through his hair. I tried to concentrate on his answer, but I couldn't stop looking at him. Every inch of him. He lay beside me with one knee bent. I traced the sculpted lines of his abdomen. His body was covered with a fine dusting of dark hair. I traced the swell of his hips, ran my hand over the corded muscle of his thigh, then brought myself back up. I couldn't stand not touching him.

"I have to get you out of here."

"I need to be where you are." The words flew out of my mouth before my brain even caught up. It was true though. I didn't just want to be near Mal, I *needed* to be. As if his body provided a different kind of sustenance.

He turned to me, resting on his elbow. He traced lazy circles around my shoulder, then a line down between my breasts, giving me goosebumps.

"I know. I should have waited before marking you. I just couldn't help it. It *had* to happen."

I nodded. I knew exactly what he meant. My hand went to the small wound he'd given me at the base of my neck. He bit me, leaving a crescent shaped mark on my skin. It didn't hurt though. In fact, it had already healed, leaving a raised scar that I traced with my fingers. Touching it like that sent a shiver of pleasure through me. It connected me to Mal like a new erogenous zone. His brand.

"You've changed me," I said. "No. Maybe not changed. It feels like you woke something up inside me that I hadn't realized was there. Imprinting. I didn't know . . . I mean. Is that what this is?"

Mal shrugged. "It's like that for me too, Laura. I thought I'd felt it before . . . with someone else. But with you, it's different." He pulled me close, cradling my head against his chest as he smoothed the damp hair out of my face. I looked up at him. His eyes filled with tenderness as he held me. He parted his lips, about to say something. But, he held back. My heart raced along with his.

I couldn't read his mind. It wasn't that kind of connection, but I think I knew what he might have said. I was starting to think it myself. The bond between us was biological. I called it an imprint, and that was perhaps the closest thing in nature I could compare it to. But, biology was one thing; my heart was something different.

I was falling in love with Mal Devane. Hard. And yet, it was all too new. I couldn't give voice to it for fear it was too soon for both of us. I bit my lip and nuzzled deeper into him.

"There's one thing though," I said, trying to find a way to ask some of these questions without offending him or sounding ignorant. Well, I was ignorant. The scientist in me had a thousand questions. Ones I knew I should have asked before we took things as far as we did. Again though, the head is one thing, and hearts and desires are something else.

"You can ask me anything, Princess."

"The way you are. Have you always been like this? Or did someone bite you too? Is it an infection or congenital?"

Mal smiled. "It's not an infection. It's in my DNA. I can't make you like me just by marking you. We're mated, but you won't be able to shift like I do. Not unless you already have recessive were DNA in you already. Even then, it would take more than just my mark to shift you. Your blood would need to mix with other weres."

His face darkened, and for a moment it felt hard to breathe. Other weres? The idea of letting another man near me, let alone sharing something like what I had with Mal, made my blood run cold. My pulse quickened, and I realized instantly it was Mal reacting to the thought as well.

"You're *mine*, Laura. No matter what. I don't plan on sharing you. I'll never make that mistake again."

His eyes went to some far off place. Attuned to his moods as I quickly became, I knew he was thinking of the other woman and whatever led him to exile from Wild Lake. I reached up and ran my thumb across his forehead, smoothing away the furrowed lines of worry there. Whatever happened to him in the past, whatever put that darkness in his eyes, I wanted to wipe it away for good. He was here with me now. A simmering rage rose within me too. I hated the thought that anyone or anything had caused him pain. He'd sworn to protect me. I wanted to protect him too.

He leaned back and smiled. "Didn't take much to bring the wild thing out of you, now did it?"

I playfully slapped at his chest. He took my hand, threading his fingers through mine. Strong hands. Hands that held and protected me. Fingers that played across my skin and worked the most sensitive parts of me, making my body sing for his. I traced the thin blue line of one of the veins across the top of his hand leading to his wrist. My wheels started to spin. What I wouldn't give to put some of Mal's cells under a microscope.

He must have seen my thoughts written on my face. Feeling bashful all of a sudden, a slow blush warmed my cheeks.

"I can't help it. I just have so many questions. You said we're mated. But, I mean . . . I don't want a baby. At least, not yet."

Mal smiled and kissed the top of my head. "I don't either. Bad timing. Though I sure as hell don't mind practicing with you. But, before you could become pregnant, I'd have to mark you many more times."

I nuzzled against him, liking the sound of that. A lot.

"Would the babies be like you or me?"

Mal threaded his fingers through mine and brought my hand to his lips. "Like me, most likely. That's the only thing that's keeping my kind from completely dying out. About ninety-nine percent of our offspring are male. It's been like that for about a hundred years."

Fresh excitement prickled along my spine. Again, the budding scientist in me wanted to dive into this with both feet.

"Do you know why? I mean has anyone ever tried to figure it out? God, there could be so many reasons. Genetic markers that . . ."

Mal interrupted my train of thought with a kiss. "God, do you realize how sexy you look when you're mind's buzzing like that? Don't worry, Princess, if I have anything to do with it, you'll have all the time in the world to study me. For now, we need to get back inside and check on Luke."

God. With everything that had happened in the last hour, I'd almost forgotten about Luke. It had been too easy to forget about everything that wasn't Mal and the way he made me feel.

Mal stood up and held a hand out to me. He let out a devilish laugh as he watched me gingerly pick myself up off the ground.

"Saddle-sore, are you?"

"Your fault."

Mal wagged his thick brows at me. He reached out and swatted my ass, making fresh desire course through me. I couldn't explain it, but soon I knew I'd have a burning need for him again that would drive out any other thought. For now, though, I needed to focus.

I crossed my arms in front of my naked breasts. My clothes were torn, soiled, soaked, and strewn halfway through the woods.

"I'll find you something to wear when we get inside," he said.

"Good. But you expect me to walk in there buck naked with Luke laying right there?"

"He's a wolf right now. Unless you're a piece of red meat, he's not interested. He's probably still unconscious anyway. And you'll walk behind me.

I gave him side eye and shrugged, but let him tuck my body behind his as he opened the door. He swung it open and I peered out from behind Mal's shoulder, still feeling self-conscious about my nudity in front of another werewolf despite Mal's reassurances.

"Son of a bitch!" Every muscle in Mal's body tensed beneath my fingertips.

Luke was in front of the fireplace, just where we'd left him. But, he was struggling to get to his feet. The wolf was gone. Luke turned, and I came face to face with the man. He stood naked before us, his body glistening with sweat. With great effort, he raised his uninjured arm and pointed a quaking finger straight at us. He said one word that struck terror through my heart.

"Die."

Chapter Seventeen

TIME FROZE for a moment as I stared at Luke. He was big. Nearly as big as Mal. But, his hair was light brown, wavy, falling to his shoulders. He had a thick, unkempt beard that hung down well past his chin. He was all lean muscle and sinew, covered in grime. Even as a man, he seemed more wild than human, like some sort of caveman.

"Shit." Mal reacted while I stood dumbfounded. Luke made a wild lunge for me. His green eyes fixed on mine, and his still held the bloodlust I'd seen when his wolf came at me yesterday. Mal dropped low and wrapped his arms around Luke's core, pinning one arm to his side. Luke had to be fueled purely by adrenalin, as he didn't look like he had the strength to stand, let alone fight. Mal twisted his body, flipping Luke over his shoulder in a wrestling move.

Luke's movements were halting, ungainly, as if he couldn't remember how to work his limbs. He scratched and clawed at Mal's back but didn't make solid contact. Mal had him on his back and pressed one knee into his chest, pinning him down.

"Laura! The cabinet under the sink. Rope. Get it!"

I ran to the kitchen, found the rope, and grabbed a knife from the counter. I uncoiled the rope and thrust it into Mal's outstretched hand. Luke twisted and kicked beneath him, his eyes cloudy and unfocused. They flashed from wolf to man and back again. Luke's flesh rolled and the cabin filled with a sickening popping noise of bones going in and out of joint.

"Stay with me," Mal said, his voice deep and commanding. "Don't you fucking shift!"

Luke screamed in agony. The effort of being either wolf *or* man sapped what little strength he had from him. His shoulder wound opened again and blood poured out.

With quick skill and strength, Mal wound the rope around Luke's legs and his uninjured arm, hog-tying him. Then, he took another length of rope and tied Luke's injured arm flat to his body. Luke thrashed and hissed, baring his teeth as he struggled both to free himself from the bindings and to give in to the urge to shift back to the wolf.

Mal moved off of Luke and cupped his face in his hands. "Luke. Dammit. Look at me. Look at my eyes. Fight. Do you fucking hear me? Stay here."

Luke growled, gritting his teeth so hard bone scraped against bone. He foamed at the mouth and blood filled his right eye as he strained hard enough to break a tiny vessel within it.

"What's happening to him?" I stayed pressed against the wall. Luke was in no position to do me harm, but I knew on instinct if I stepped into his line of sight, his agony could worsen. He was one of Asher's soldiers. He'd been sent out to kill me. He warred with the command. I could see it in his face as veins popped out along his temple.

"He broke free. Just for a moment. Asher's trying to call him back."

"What do we do?"

"Wait," Mal said, his own voice mirroring the agony Luke must have felt. "See if he's got the strength to fight it off."

Luke's face changed from red to white to a pale shade of green. His brows lengthened and started to grow together as the wolf fought to get out.

"What if he doesn't? Mal? If Asher's got a hold of him, won't he lead him right to us?"

"I'll stop it if I have to."

I meant to ask him how, but I saw the answer in Mal's curled fist as he held it over Luke's face. Luke jerked his head back, struggling to meet Mal's eyes. I sank to the floor, hugging my knees as I watched the horrific spectacle.

As he thrashed against his bindings, Luke found the strength to hold his head still and focus on Mal, just for a moment at least. Asher may have been his Alpha, but Mal's force was strong.

"H-help me," he said in a ragged whisper that tore at my heart. "M-make . . . it . . . s-stop!"

Mal pounded his fist against the ground. "Where is he? Tell me where to find his den. I swear to God I'll kill him, Luke. I'll get you home to Wild Lake where you belong. You and the others. But, I need you to help me do that."

Luke shook his head. "C-can't. T-too strong. Have to go."

"No! Luke. You stay with me!"

"He'll m-make me h-hurt you. K-kill your g-girl. H-he knows. W-wants you to watch her d-die s-s-slow."

Now it was Mal having difficulty keeping his wolf at bay. He threw his head back and let out a growl loud enough to rattle the windows.

"Mal!" I shouted, knowing on instinct if he couldn't keep his shit together either, we were fucked. He turned and looked back at me with wild eyes. A muscle twitched in his jaw, then he turned back to Luke.

"Where is he?" He shook Luke hard enough to make him yelp. The pain in his shoulder had to be searing.

"H-help me!"

"Goddammit, I'm trying! What do you want me to do?"

Luke's body went very still. It was only a fraction of a second, but he found the strength to make his eyes clear. He focused them on Mal as he cradled Luke's head in his hands. Luke shut his eyes tight then opened them again. In that brief space, the wolf inside him had quieted. Luke leaned forward. When he spoke, his voice was strong and dark.

"Kill me."

Then hell seemed to break loose within him once again. His eyes clouded over and blazed green, the irises receded leaving only the beast's. Mal didn't have to tell me what could happen if Luke shifted back completely. He was awake now. Only the man had the strength of reason to fight against Asher's control. The minute he became fully wolf again, Asher would know where to find him. Where to find us.

"Fuck!" Mal shouted, throwing his head back again.

"Mal!" My own voice ripped from my throat, terror rising.

Mal cocked his fist again and brought it down hard across Luke's face, shattering the small bones in Luke's nose. Blood sprayed across his forearm. But the light went out of Luke's eyes and his head lolled back. Injured as he was, he shifted quickly, almost peacefully back into the wolf. His body heaved with unsteady breaths, but he was out cold. Mal adjusted the bindings, immobilizing Luke if he woke up again.

I grabbed the first aid kit and went to Mal's side. I took a length of gauze and wiped the blood off Mal's arm. He stiffened but let me do it. He buried his face in his hand and sank down on the floor.

"Fuck," he said quietly.

I looked back at Luke. He would have ripped me to pieces in the woods, but now I understood. God, the torment he endured under Asher.

"He needs to die," Mal said, echoing my thoughts. "I swear to God, Laura. Asher is never going to get near you again."

"I know. But, Mal. I get it now. *Really* get it. You have to help Luke. And you think the rest of Asher's pack are like him? They're suffering inside like that?"

Mal closed his eyes and slowly nodded. "I think so. The last skirmish we had with Asher's pack, we killed the last of the wolves truly loyal to him. All that's left are those who I think want to return to Wild Lake if given the chance."

"So what do you need?"

Mal let out a humorless laugh. "My own army."

"I'm serious."

"I need to know where he goes when he sleeps. He's got numbers, so the only way I can kill him is if I take him by surprise. The minute he's dead, hell . . . the minute he's unconscious, his hold over the others will break."

"So why don't they just sneak off when he's sleeping?"

"Not that kind of unconscious. Asher's exerting total influence over the pack. They sleep when he commands them to. They're easier to control in wolf form. You just saw that with Luke. He isn't letting them shift back to human form. God, Luke looked like he hasn't shifted in months. It's going to kill him eventually. It's already driving him mad."

I shuddered. Asher was keeping the rest of his pack imprisoned within themselves. It was torture for them. Hell.

"I need to know where he's going before he goes there. I need the impossible," Mal said. The instant he did, something clicked in place. My mind raced as an idea formed in my head. Shit. Oh, shit.

Mal narrowed his eyes at me, sensing my pulse quicken. "Laura? What is it?"

I stood up, tearing my hand through my hair I paced in front of him.

"Laura?" Mal reached up and grabbed my wrist, turning me to face him.

"I know what you need," I said, my heart beat so fast I gasped out my words. "I know how to help you see where Asher's going before he gets there. Well . . . kind of, anyway."

Mal cocked his head. I pressed my hands against his chest and smiled wide. "I have a plan. You're really, *really* not going to like it, but it could work."

Chapter Eighteen

"NO WAY. NO FUCKING WAY." Mal stormed through the cabin. He'd knocked chairs over, broken a mason jar in the kitchen, and kicked a rug across the room.

"Mal, it's a solid plan. You *need* me to do this. You said so yourself."

"What I *need* is for you to do what I say."

I folded my arms in front of me. "Is that how this works now? We're mated so I have to follow your every command? Fuck that, Mal. I didn't sign up for that."

He was on me in one quick stride. He curled his fingers around my shoulders and jerked me forward, not hard, but forceful enough to get my attention. He crushed his lips to mine and kissed me. Heat rose within me as my body responded to his. God, even when he was unreasonable, I wanted him so badly now, and he knew it. He could use my own urges against me. Part of me wanted him to.

Yeah. He had me. The mark at the back of my neck flared hot

to match the pulsation lower down. It had been several hours since I'd first told him about my idea. I'd been fighting the need to throttle him for being obstinate and wanting to let him bend me over the table and fuck my brains out.

"You know it's a good idea. The best one we've got."

"We? This is my fight, Laura. Me and Asher."

I flapped my hands and smacked them against my thighs. A fairly ineffective gesture, as I was wearing one of Mal's flannel shirts. It hung down almost to my knees and my hands disappeared inside it. I had the fleeting thought that after all of this, I hoped life with Malcolm Devane included a washer and dryer.

"Right. But in case you forgot, my name is mixed up in all of this. I figure the best way to fix that is to get rid of Asher. Once Flood doesn't have his protection, I'm thinking you and the rest of the pack can . . . uh . . . exert some influence over that fucker and get him to change his story."

Mal reared back, staring blankly at the wall. He opened and closed his mouth like a fish. Then, he fixed his eyes back on me and smirked. "Okay. That part is actually not a half bad idea. The rest of it though? Laura, I am not letting you march back to that camp."

"Well, I wasn't exactly talking about marching. I was thinking sneaky, a little more stealth-like."

His raised brow didn't exactly instill confidence.

"Mal, come on. You said you needed to know Asher's movements without getting close enough where he can track you. Well, I can do that. I told you. We tag Luke and set him free. He leads us straight to Asher and shazam, element of surprise."

I crossed my arms in front of me and leaned against the wall. Mal shook his head and pressed his thumb into his eye, rubbing hard.

"I hate it," he muttered.

I smiled. "You hate that I'm right."

He growled, but the fight had gone out of him. I pushed myself off the wall and went to him, sliding my arms around his waist. As I pressed myself against him, I felt the slow rise of his erection against my stomach. An answering heat flared within me.

"Is that ever going to stop?" I asked, starting to lose the ability to think straight. Before I even knew what I was doing, I dropped to my knees in front of him and worked on the button of his jeans. "I mean. Mal, I want you *all* the time."

His erection sprang free before me, huge and hard.

He laughed, low and sexy. "It's going to be urgent like this for a few weeks, probably. It's called the Rise. It eases when we mate and I mark you again and again. I'm sorry if it's torture for you, but I gotta say I sure as hell don't mind."

I slapped his ass, but the fight had gone out of me too. Mal knew what we needed to do and recognized it as the best plan he was likely to get. Smiling, I gently gripped the base of his cock and drew my lips over his shaft. He ran his fingers through my hair and pulled me down the length of him. I looked up at him just as he threw his head back in ecstasy as I started to suck.

Torture. Delicious torture. If that's what being marked by my Alpha meant, I sure as hell didn't mind either.

WE LEFT at just after midnight. Luke was in a deep sleep, tied up by the hearth. Mal gauged the rest of the pack likely slept now too. It afforded us the cover of darkness, plus I knew Flood and the others would have turned in for the night as well.

Mal had a Range Rover of his own hidden deeper in the woods. We drove in silence back to the G.L.U. outpost, my heart beating a wild rhythm the entire time. I'd fought so hard to convince Mal to try my plan, but now that we were actually doing it, my confidence leached out of me.

I didn't want to ever see Flood again. Asher had a pack of werewolves looking to trap me and kill me slow. Mal reached across the console and squeezed my hand, sensing my apprehension.

"I'll be everywhere, Laura. If anything happens, you won't even have to scream. I'll know you're in trouble."

"And you'll keep watch while I go in?"

"You bet your ass I will. You take the keys. I'll be able to sense more if I shift. When it's time to high-tail it out of there, you drive."

"Got it. Your paws probably wouldn't reach the pedals."

He chuffed a growl and squeezed my hand again. I meant to crack another joke, anything to still the wildness of my heart, but we made the last turn to the trail leading up to the outpost. Mal killed the lights and the engine. We decided it was better to leave the Range Rover hidden and go in on foot.

I gave Mal a nod and quietly stepped out of the car, closing the door behind me, careful not to slam it. Mal stepped out and peeled off his clothes, folding them neatly and placing them in the back seat. He came around the car and stood in front of me. Under a half moon, his eyes glinted. I reached up and ran my hands along his shoulders, marveling still at his form, even now. He leaned down and kissed me quick.

"Nothing fancy," he said. "You go to the lab, get what you need, and get out. You see anyone, anyone at all, you run. You can't trust Cam or anyone else there. You know that, right? No matter what they might say to you."

I nodded. "I get it. I'm on my own."

Mal closed his fingers around my wrists and pulled me to him, his eyes flashed fiercely. "No. You are not. You have me. You'll never be alone again."

Warmth flooded me as his strong heartbeat rose to match mine. He dropped my wrists and stepped back. He let out a hard breath and looked toward the moon. Then, his body dropped and shifted with speed and power that took my breath away. The black wolf stood before me. He lowered his head once then tore off into the woods.

"Right," I said to no one. "Time to get her done."

I squared my shoulders and took the first steps toward the cabins.

Chapter Nineteen

THE CAMP WAS dark and quiet. I didn't dare walk through the main thoroughfare. Instead, I kept to the woods, fighting brambles and sticks. Mal circled around me, panting. Energy hummed through his body and seemed to transmit to mine. He was keyed up but exhilarated. I understood exactly why. We were doing something. Trying to take charge of a situation that had us both pinned down for days. He ran ahead, cutting a zig-zag path through the woods making sure the coast was clear. Only the humming crickets and the occasional hooting owl remarked on our progress.

My heart beat in my throat as I stepped out of the relative safety of the brush and entered the main compound. I pressed my back flat against the mess hall cabin. All the lights in the camp were dark except for a yellow flicker coming from one of the cabins at the opposite end from where I stood. I knew it housed a few of the grad students from another school. Flood's cabin and Cam's were completely dark. I'd have to pass right in front of Flood's cabin to get where I needed to go. Even with Mal prowling nearby, cold terror flooded my veins.

The black Jeep was parked back in front of the lab cabin. My heart fluttered when I saw it. I hoped Flood and the cops figured I was long gone by now. Mal worried we might be running into a trap if the rangers decided to put people in place to watch the camp. But, the grounds looked as isolated as ever. Good for me, bad for Asher.

Taking a steeling breath, I moved between the cabins, ducking low if I passed by a dark window. A pair of yellow eyes flashed across the thoroughfare from the deepest part of the woods. This time, they gave me comfort and renewed confidence. Mal was here and I wasn't alone.

When I came to the lab, I stopped. Peering through the window, I couldn't see a thing. The place was pitch dark and empty. For the first time since I came up with the plan, I started to feel bold. I looked back toward Mal and gave him a slow nod. He receded deeper into the woods; he wanted to circle the perimeter to make sure none of Asher's pack were on the move.

I tried the door and found the lab locked. I expected this. Luckily, I still had the key Flood gave me when we first came out here. I felt my way along the door jamb and found the keyhole. I slipped my key into the lock and turned it gently. The door opened soundlessly and I stepped inside. I crouched low, planning to crawl through the lab with the small Maglite Mal gave me between my teeth. That way, if anyone walked by or looked toward the lab from their window, they wouldn't see me or the bobbing light within.

I felt my way along the cold, steel tables. We kept the deer tags and tracking devices in the back. I hoped to God Flood hadn't used them all. We'd tagged fifteen fawns and had twenty microchips. Five to spare. My fingers closed around the metal handle to the drawer where we kept the equipment. Slowly, I opened it, pointing the flashlight straight down.

Jackpot! Flood may have been a lecherous asshole, but his touch of O.C.D. came in handy tonight. All five microchip kits neatly lined the bottom of the drawer. I grabbed two of them and put them carefully in my backpack. That was the easy part. I closed the drawer, lifting it from the bottom to keep it from noisily scraping against the sides. Next, I needed to find one of the laptops. There were five of them as well. Flood had issued one to me, one to Cam, and used one himself. The other two he kept in storage for backup. I prayed he wouldn't notice one missing. If he did, he was smart enough to piece together who might have taken one and what I was up to. I had no idea how much contact he and Asher maintained. But, if Asher came back here and told Flood that Luke was AWOL, we were sunk.

I walked back to the large metal storage locker at the back of the room. Flood may have had a touch of O.C.D., but it didn't mean he wasn't careless. He never kept the thing locked. I pulled up on the metal handle, sliding the latch to the side. I got the door open an inch before I remembered the horrific screeching noise the rusted hinges always made when we swung the door open. I froze, crouching low.

Shit. There was no way to get the thing open all the way without the screech. Sticking the flashlight between my teeth again, I slid my hand into the gap I'd made. The laptops were on the middle shelf. I reached back, holding the door steady as my fingers felt along the shelf until I could find the outline of one of the thin, 11-inch notebooks. Carefully, I lifted it, turning it sideways so I could fit it through the gap in the door.

I just had to hope the thing was fully charged. Mal's cabin had no electricity. The laptops had eleven hours of battery life.

Once I had the laptop in my pack, I reached into the locker again and felt around for the extra battery packs we kept, hoping between those and the juice in the laptop itself, we'd have all the time we needed. If worst came to worst, I could rig something to charge it from the Range Rover's battery.

Taking a deep breath, I closed the locker door gently and zipped up my pack. Almost over. I heard laughter outside and my heart froze. I clicked off the flashlight. With the sparse moonlight, I still had enough light to avoid crashing into any of the tables as I crawled along the floor and headed for the front door. I wished to God this place had another exit. Unless I wanted to chance crawling out the window, I'd have to wait until whoever was out there walked by. Unfortunately, the riskiest part of this plan was yet to come. I'd have to pass by Flood's cabin one more time to get to the woods and the meeting point Mal set up.

I heard more giggling and the rustling of clothes. I crept up and peered out the bottom of the window. Two of the grad students from the other school leaned up against the side of the mess hall where the shadows were darkest. Bad news, they were two potential witnesses if I couldn't make it out quietly. Good news, they were both currently more interested in making out than anything else going on around them.

I stayed low to the ground hopefully out of their line of sight as I exited the lab and made my way out of the camp. There was only Flood's cabin up ahead then the great expanse of the forest beyond it. Now, that forest meant safety. *Home.*

The thought flared in my mind unbidden. Home. Up until a few days ago, I still half thought of Green Bluff, California as home. My family. My parents. My brothers and sisters. I hadn't really seen any of them in almost eight months. I loved them. They were part of me. But I'd left so much of that behind.

Coming from a family of nine, I'd been raised to be independent. As we all got older, we could go for months, even years in some cases without seeing one another. But, family was family, and the bond was still strong. An ache filled my heart when I thought about what my parents must be going through if they'd heard any of the accusations thrown at me. With my phone dead, I had no idea if they'd even tried to contact me.

The ache in my heart turned to rage as I got closer to Flood's cabin. Doubt started to creep in as well. If we managed to get the tracker embedded in Luke's skin, if we had enough battery life and luck, we'd be able to see where Luke went. It was a good plan but based on a lot of those what-ifs. The biggest piece scared me the most. Once Mal figured out where Asher was holed up, what then? Even with Luke injured, it would still be four strong werewolves against just Mal. God, for the first time, I *wished* his mark would turn me. Maybe then I could be strong enough to fight by his side. The thought of harm coming to him made my blood turn cold. He'd warned me Asher might not stop trying to hurt me. That I could take sanctuary at Wild Lake. But, the idea of not having Mal by my side tore at me. Now that I'd taken him into my heart, I flat out couldn't imagine going back to a life without him. It had happened so fast, so intensely, and yet, I knew it was real.

Another idea sprang up in my mind. Maybe there was a way. He had to try to take out Asher without hurting any of the rest of his pack. Just like the microchip trackers, there might be an answer right here under my nose.

The tranquilizer guns.

I knew I was a good enough shot to use them. But Mal would have to agree to let me get close enough to do it. I knew exactly how much he'd hate the idea, just like this one.

I was thirty yards from the edge of the forest with only Flood's quiet cabin between me and relative safety. Mal stepped into view, his eyes flashing, his dark fur raised along his back. I looked back to Flood's cabin. He kept the dart guns with him, claiming it was a liability issue with the university. He couldn't store them in a common area.

Before I even knew what I was doing, I stepped onto the porch of Flood's cabin. Mal let out a low growl of warning. I felt his pulse quicken, thundering between my ears. But, there was no time. I was here. Just a few feet away from what might be our best chance to stop Asher and Flood once and for all. The side of Flood's building shielded me from the students making out across the thoroughfare. But, if Mal came out of the woods, he would be in their direct line of sight. I was the only one with a quick chance of grabbing the dart guns and getting the hell out of here.

I peered through the window. Flood slept in the center of his bed, face down, snoring. I could see the long tranquilizer gun leaning against the far wall. He kept a box of darts behind it. It was so close. Flood stirred, snorting in his sleep, but he didn't wake.

Carefully, I turned the latch to his door. A flash of white caught my eye as Mal bared his teeth and started to walk slowly toward me. I put a hand up and pressed my lips together. I gestured one minute with my raised index finger and opened Flood's door the rest of the way. Mercifully, it didn't creak. But, I had to close it behind me to keep it from slamming shut. Now, I was alone in the room with Flood. If he woke. If he came after me, there'd be no way to get out of this without Mal ripping his throat out and then everyone would know where we were and what we'd come for.

On second thought, maybe this was a colossally bad idea.

Chapter Twenty

I STEPPED GINGERLY across the room, barely allowing myself to breathe as I headed for the gun and darts. Even if I managed to get out of here before he woke, he'd probably figure out the thing was gone. But, if we were lucky, it wouldn't matter. We still had hours before sunlight. Plenty of time to release Luke and start tracking him. Plus, there was a good chance Flood wouldn't notice the gun was gone right away. He didn't use it every day. In fact, I'd only ever seen him with it once. There was hope and more than a good shot we'd have a day or more.

I leaned down slowly and grabbed the box of darts, holding them steady so they wouldn't rattle. Then, I closed my fingers around the barrel of the gun and walked back to the door.

Flood stirred. He rolled to his back and his eyes opened. I froze, pressing myself flat against the wall and into the shadows. He rubbed a hand over his groin and I saw the telltale tenting of his sheets. Gross. The guy had a hard on and was dreaming about God knows what. A few seconds ticked by, and he seemed to settle back down.

I took a deep breath and held it as I made my way back toward the door. I didn't want to turn my back on Flood, but I had to turn the latch and open the door. Slowly, deliberately, I eased my way out. I grimaced as I stepped through the door and closed it soundlessly behind me.

Red menace stared me in the face when I turned around.

Mal's black wolf stood an inch away, his back arched, his tail up, and his frightening row of deadly teeth bared.

I put a finger to my lips. I waved the dart gun in front of me. But, in this state, Mal was incapable of human reason. He saw threat and danger and me in the middle. I put a hand out and laid it flat on his head. He flinched, but didn't advance. I pointed to the woods and mouthed, "Let's go!"

Mal looked behind me once. I recognized the same bloodlust clouding his eyes as I'd seen in Luke. But Mal's was directed at Flood. Yeah. Time to get us both the hell out of here before he ripped Flood's throat out for good. As much as the idea had appeal, I still needed the bastard if I had any hope of clearing my name.

I tugged a tuft of hair on Mal's back and started toward the woods. He growled again but fell into step. He let out a sharp whine that I knew was meant for me. In wolf-speak, I think he'd just said something like, "Just wait until I get you home."

We ran the rest of the way back to the Range Rover. On the way in, stealth had been the key. On the way out, it was speed. Mal ran ahead and around me, watching the perimeter. When we got to the vehicle, I opened the passenger door and climbed in the driver's side. I expected Mal to shift and hop in beside me, but he just froze in front of me.

"Get in!" I whispered, still worried our voices might somehow carry all the way back to the cabins.

Mal pawed the ground but didn't otherwise move. He narrowed his eyes and let out a chuff. He bobbed his head up and down toward the Range Rover. He didn't speak in words, and yet somehow I understood him perfectly. He wanted me to drive back to the cabin without him.

I didn't like it. Not one bit. But, I'd altered the plan on the fly back at the outpost, so I couldn't exactly give him shit for doing it now. I let out a sigh and shut the passenger door. Then, I climbed into the driver's seat and started the engine. By the time I looked back up, Mal had torn off ahead of me. Whatever was going on with him, he clearly wanted to stay in wolf form. It unsettled me more than a little; it meant he wasn't certain we were in the clear yet. I put the car in gear and headed back to Mal's cabin, hoping I'd find him there when I arrived.

WHEN I PULLED up to Mal's cabin, it was still eerily quiet. I knew I had to take that as a good sign. I grabbed the dart gun and my backpack and headed inside. Luke was still out cold in front of the fireplace, tied up just as we'd left him. For the first time since we'd set out on this caper, my breath came easier.

Mal hadn't come back but I knew this part of the plan was all me anyway. I fired up the laptop and took out one of the microchip kits. With shaking fingers, I loaded the chip into the syringe, scanned it and stepped over to Luke.

His breathing was shallow but steady. A red patch stained the center of the bandages we'd changed before we left, but it wasn't getting any wider. It looked like the bleeding had finally stopped. I grabbed the loose skin at the scruff of his neck and positioned the needle.

The front door flew open Mal stood there, wearing the pair of jeans he'd put in the Range Rover and a fearsome stare.

"Not now," I said, popping the plastic cap off the syringe with my teeth. He looked ready to rip my head off.

Mal came to my side and put a hand on Luke's back as I plunged the needle into his skin and ejected the chip. I pulled the needle out and smoothed back the hair over the puncture wound I made.

"How long before it starts to transmit?" Mal's tone was ominous.

"Pretty much now if we're lucky. I need to fire up the laptop and launch the software. Once that's up and running, we're good to go."

"Good," Mal said, his voice flat and devoid of emotion. It unsettled me. I knew he was mad about my stunt at the cabin, but he was going to have to see the necessity of it sooner or later.

"Get that thing running," he said, gesturing to the laptop. "I'm taking him out of here."

Before I could question it, Mal scooped Luke's limp form up in his arms. God, he was so strong. Even sick as he was, Luke the wolf wasn't a lightweight. Mal picked him up as if he were a feather.

"I'll be back. Luke's going to remember where this cabin is, but I'm going to lay him down where he attacked you. Hopefully, he'll be disoriented enough to give us some time."

Time for what, I wanted to ask, but the stony expression in

Mal's eyes quieted my questions. God, he seemed really mad at me. I nodded and started firing up the laptop. Without another word, Mal carried Luke out of the cabin and disappeared from sight.

I set the laptop on one of the chairs and sat cross-legged in front of it, waiting for the software to boot. We had a few hours until daylight. If things were business as usual at the outpost, Flood would start logging his data at daybreak. I wanted to get as much info as I could before he figured out there was an extra tracker running.

It took only a few seconds for the GPS map to load. It filled the screen in deep green and blue, marking the dense forest, rivers, and lakes throughout the Manistee National Park.

"Come on!" I gently tapped the side of the screen, knowing full well that would do nothing other than make me feel better. As the minutes ticked by, the small red dots marking our specimens started to populate the map. I was looking for Tag 16: That would be Luke.

The screen hung up twice. This far out in the woods, the cell signal from the old air card we used would cut out. For a moment, I thought I'd never get a clear signal. Finally, though, a fast moving red dot flashed across the screen.

"There you are!"

I went into settings and changed the dot from red to orange so we could distinguish it faster from the fawns Flood tracked. It would only show up that way on this laptop, so there was no risk of Flood picking it out.

"God, he's so fast." With Mal carrying him, the dot was moving at more than twenty miles an hour on foot. I checked the settings twice to make sure I was reading that right. Then, abruptly, the orange dot stopped moving. I checked the coordinates. Sure enough, Mal had him roughly in the area where Luke had come after me, about a mile north of the ranger station.

A few more seconds ticked by. The orange dot pulsed strong but didn't move. Luke was bedded down, probably still unconscious. The longer he was, the better. Mal needed time to get out of there and back to me. The moment I thought it, my heart fluttered. Mal was out there. Exposed. With a pack of four strong werewolves hunting him and wanting him dead.

Though he hadn't told me the plan, I knew we'd need to be on the move, and quickly. We couldn't risk the chance that Luke would be able to lead Asher and the pack straight back here when he woke. I started packing up what I could. If we were out in the open, Mal could hunt for himself, but I'd need to eat. I stuffed my backpack with energy bars and filled three large canteens with water from the well. I took the tranquilizer darts out of the box and found plastic bags to seal them in case we had to travel through water again. I did the same for the 12 gauge shells. I packed everything into the back of the Range Rover and waited for Mal to come back to me, my heart pounding with anticipation the entire time.

Four hours went by before he came back. He'd tell me later that he zig-zagged and circled back several times to throw off any trail Luke or the others might pick up. It would buy us time, but we couldn't stay at the cabin anymore. Mal was strangely quiet as he helped me pack the rest of our necessities. Finally, after about an hour of the silent treatment, I couldn't take another second.

"What's the matter with you?" I stood with my hands on my hips at the back of the car. Mal had just finished packing a tent and shoved in on top of the rest of the supplies.

He looked at me, eyes glowering, but didn't answer. I stepped forward and put my hands on his chest. "Talk to me! You've been acting like an asshole ever since we got back from Flood's camp. What the hell is the matter with you?"

A muscle in his neck jumped while every other muscle in his body went rigid. He put his hands up and gripped me by the shoulders.

"You put yourself at risk. You disobeyed me."

I reared back as if he'd slapped me. "I what?"

"You went into . . . *his* . . . cabin. You put yourself close to him. God. I can still smell him on you."

"Again . . . what? Mal. Think. We need the dart gun. There's no place else to get one like that in a hurry. We've got a pack of wolves after us and you want to bring four of them back alive."

"I can't shoot a gun if I'm a wolf, Laura."

I literally sputtered for a second at that. "Yeah. But I can, Mal. I've told you before and you've seen the evidence. I'm a good shot. I grew up hunting with five brothers."

Mal's grip on my arms tightened and he shook me hard enough to make my teeth rattle. "You think I'm letting you get anywhere near that pack? Near Asher? You're going to show me how the trackers work, and then you're going to get in that car and head for Wild Lake and wait for me. That's what's happening."

I was thunderstruck finally hearing his plan. He wanted to send me away. He planned to take on Asher's pack all by himself. First, rage boiled through me. We were in this together. Mal's fate was my fate. He'd been telling me that from the beginning and I knew it was true in my gut. But, as I looked at him, standing with his legs slightly apart, fire raging behind his eyes, I sensed something else too. In addition to whatever macho, testosterone-fueled, Alpha wolf reasoning he had for trying to bench me, I could feel the desperate fear coiled deep inside him. I stepped back and he loosened his grip on my arms. His chest heaved with his hot breath.

"Mal," I said, my voice cracking. "You need me."

His nostrils flared and he curled his right hand into a fist then smashed it against the door of the Range Rover, making a circular dent. He pointed a finger at me, his words came out slow. "I will not risk you. I will not lose you."

The emotion behind his words tore at my heart as something clicked into place. Mal had already lost everything. His pack. His home. Everything. He'd been on his own for months suffering from a different kind of torture than Luke, but it had to be torture just the same. Wolves weren't meant to live alone. *My* wolf wasn't meant to live alone.

I stepped forward, placing trembling fingers on his chest. His muscles tensed beneath my touch, but he didn't pull away. Instead, he closed his fingers around my wrist and encircled my waist with his other arm.

"I will not lose you, Laura."

I swallowed hard and looked up at him. The fire in his eyes masked the desolation he'd had to live with for so long. "I can't lose you either, Mal. Not now. But you're *not* alone anymore. And I can help you. If you try to take on Asher's pack by yourself, you're going to die. Strong as you are, you're outnumbered five to one. I don't know what happened to you back at Wild Lake, but you've been sent on an impossible mission. You can't take out Asher alone. Not with the rest of the pack under his control."

"Nothing matters except keeping you safe. Do you understand? I don't have to survive, but you do."

"I don't accept that!" My voice rose an octave, my tone bordering on hysteria. "You stand there telling me how you can't live without me. Well, I can't live without you anymore either. You knew what would happen when you marked me. I don't want to go to Wild Lake. Not unless you're by my side."

Mal shut his eyes tight, and his body vibrated with a steady rumble as he held back the wolf. When he snapped them open, I could see how much of a battle it really was. Mal's amber eyes were gone, leaving the glowing, golden eyes of the beast inside.

Heat flared through me, taking my breath away. Standing this close to him, his passion burning so bright, I had no hope of any self-control. He called what was happening to me the Rise. It was a perfect description. My body was tuned to his. As his heart beat faster, so did mine. The burning need inside me threatened to erupt, driving away all rational thought.

"I won't lose you," he said.

I shook my head. "You won't. And I won't lose you either. But we have to stay together."

Mal let out a chuff that set my blood on fire. God. He was all man, all Alpha, and all mine. "You'll do what I say. Do you understand?"

Yes. Oh, yes. I wanted him to dominate and command me. My body cried out for it. My lust seemed to short circuit all rational thought. I had just as much beast inside of me, it seemed.

"Never again," he growled. "Never again will you try something like what you did back at the camp, Laura. You're mine. Say it."

"I-I'm yours. Yes. Whatever we do, we'll do it together. No more going off on my own."

He pressed his lips to mine. His hands were all over me. My clothes felt like a prison. Warmth flooded through me and settled between my legs. With just a touch, just the tone of his voice, Mal could have me soaked and ready for him in an instant. And he knew it.

"Prove it," he said.

So I did. What happened next was rough, wild, and fast. There was no time for anything else. I ripped open the button of my jeans and pulled them down past my thighs as Mal turned me. Somehow, we were at the side of the Range Rover. He guided me down, bending me over so I stretched across the back seat, my feet planted wide on the ground. I heard Mal unbuckle his own jeans. He gave me a firm smack on the ass that made me quiver.

"Say it," he said.

"Yours," I gasped. Mal leaned forward and lifted the hair from the nape of my neck. He'd been rough before; this time, he was even rougher and my body rose to it. He sank his teeth into my scarred flesh, deepening the brand he made, the perfect blend of pleasure and pain. The mark flared hot and pulsed in time with my throbbing sex.

Then he entered me, taking no time to ease his passage. But, he didn't need to. I was already gaping open for him, slick with desire. He sheathed himself to the root. Again, pain and pleasure flooded through me as he stretched me wide and claimed me. Mal was swift this time. He coaxed me to a shattering orgasm with his fingers as he pumped inside of me. No sooner had he entered me before I felt the first, hot spurt of his seed filling me deep. It was what he needed. I'd gone against him back at the camp. I wasn't sorry for it. I knew I'd been right. And yet, Mal was my Alpha. For the first time, I understood the power of that. He would love me, protect me, treat me as his equal, but his will would not be denied. I knew I might often chafe against it. He knew it too. I could submit to him, but I could never be completely submissive all the time. It wasn't in my nature, and he knew that too. For that, he would deliver sweet punishment this way. Deliciously deserved and my body rose to it . . . craved it.

I screamed his name as he pumped the last of his seed into me and I reached the apex of my own ecstasy as he held me spread wide beneath him. He fucked me deep, each thrust an exclamation point to the unspoken command he gave. He claimed me. He owned me. He loved me. And I loved him back.

Chapter Twenty-One

WE MOVED with a singular purpose after that. I felt a new shift within me. Mal had marked me for a second time. He didn't have to tell me it meant something. I felt even more connected to him than before. I couldn't read his thoughts, not words at least, but I knew his purpose as if it were my own.

We packed up the Rover and headed away from the cabin. I chanced a look back, a forlorn feeling clouding my heart. I was reborn here. Mal had claimed me here. And I knew I would likely never see it again.

Mal drove west as I fired up the laptop. We were taking a risk as it was late afternoon now. Flood was likely also logged into the system. He wouldn't be able to detect another user, but if he saw Tag 16's signal, he'd know it was new.

"What do you see?" Mal asked.

The chip had been tracking Luke's movements for almost twelve hours. I downloaded the data and watched as the software zeroed in on one small grid in the vast forest.

"He stayed where you left him for about three hours," I said. "Then, he started moving north. Slow. He stopped three or four times it looks like. I don't know. I think he's still on his own."

I waited as the system showed me the time lapse for the next couple of hours. Luke made very little progress north. I imagined him taking slow, halting steps as he tried to find the strength to stand, let alone run.

"Wait! There!" I tapped the screen to make the grid bigger.

"What is it?"

"Three hours ago. The signal moves fast. North by northwest. He's moving along the river."

Then the orange blip came into contact with a red blip. I punched up the data. It was Tag 9, a yearling I'd chipped myself early in the summer. Then, Tag 9 disappeared.

"He's hunting!" I clapped my hands together. "Oh, shit. Poor Number Nine."

Mal pulled the car over to the side of the trail. "Show me."

I rewound the time lapse and showed Mal what I saw. He furrowed his brow and ran a thumb along his jaw.

"That was a yearling. A button buck."

Mal cocked his head to the side. I couldn't help but giggle a little as it was a purely canine expression of alarm or confusion. A slow grin spread across his face and he fisted my t-shirt and drew me to him, planting a hot kiss on my lips.

"What?" I said. I leaned into him. We'd been on the road for an hour, and I couldn't help the lustful hunger he sparked in me.

"Luke isn't strong enough to take down a buck yet. Even a small one. He's not traveling alone anymore. The pack's with him!"

My heart flipped in both excitement and fear. I expected the tracker to work, not just this well this fast. But, Luke had no idea he'd been tagged and neither did Flood or Asher as far as we knew. Their guard was down.

"Where are they now, can you tell?"

I hit the refresh button and waited for the data to update. Then, the orange blip flared to life in the top left corner of the screen. "There! It's moving slow again. Almost stationary. That's only about ten miles from here. Right along the Manistee River. There aren't any stations or outposts through there. None of the park trails either."

Mal nodded. "That's where I'd go if I were Asher. As far away from people as possible."

He pressed his foot on the gas, lurching the Rover forward. My heart raced. "Now? Aren't we going to . . . uh . . . right now?"

Mal smiled. His own pulse quickened. "The longer we wait, the worse our chances. One way or another. This ends with Asher tonight."

THE PLAN WAS simple once Mal laid it out. Well, it was my plan after all. It was just now that we were really about to execute it, I panicked a little.

"You're as safe as I can make you," Mal said.

"I know. And I'm not as worried about me as I am you. Are you sure you won't let me come in a little closer?"

"Absolutely not," Mal answered his voice firm. We'd been over the same argument about a dozen times. He went to the back of the Range Rover and pulled out a green metal tree stand kit.

"That one," I said, pointing to a large elm. It stretched tall above us with thick, sturdy branches. Mal nodded and hoisted the tree stand to his back and started to climb. He went fast, as if he were were-monkey instead of wolf. He went higher than I'd normally feel safe, but he insisted the higher the better. He hooked the stand around the thick trunk and tested his weight on it, bouncing up and down hard enough to make the tree top sway.

Then, he climbed down just as fast, suspending himself from a low branch he reached a hand out to me. I took a steadying breath and let him haul me up to the closest branch. With Mal just above me, helping me climb, I made it up to the tree stand. We were close to thirty feet off the ground, about ten more than I felt comfortable with. But, extra height meant extra time in case something went wrong.

Mal balanced on a strong branch beside me as I stepped down on the platform. With cold efficiency, he latched my safety harness around me and secured it tightly to the tree. Gripping the harness with one hand, he tested the platform again.

"It's solid," I said, checking the straps myself.

Mal nodded and leaned in to give me a quick peck on the cheek. "Sit tight. I'll be right back up." Then, he shimmied down the tree and out of sight. I heard him open and close the car door, then the tree shook as he started his ascent again. He handed me the shotgun, the tranquilizer gun, and my pack. He pulled a slim, black phone out of one of the pockets.

"This is your doomsday scenario," he said. "It's a burner, untraceable. If everything else goes to shit, you call for help."

I nodded and put the phone in my pack.

"How will I know when it's time?"

Mal smiled and leaned in to kiss me deeply again. His pulse flared inside of me, hot and steady.

"You'll know when I'm getting close. And you'll know if I'm in trouble."

"Right."

"Chances are it'll be Joe, Sam, and Dax on my tail when I run out. You remember them from that day at your camp? Three gray wolves. Asher will send his soldiers after me first. Luke's still gonna be too weak to do much damage if he even joins the fight at all. Do what you can to get a clean shot off at any of those three. You see anything with gray fur moving fast, shoot it. Red fur, hold your fire. Asher's mine."

"But, if shit does go wrong, they can climb as fast as you can, right?"

"Not in wolf form they can't. I'm betting Asher won't be willing to release them long enough to let 'em shift. Even if he does, you saw what Luke was like when he turned human again after months in his wolf. They'll be lucky to be able to put one foot in front of the other, let alone climb. And yes, Asher can climb as fast as me, but you'll have the advantage of height and more than a dozen rounds at close range. He's mad; he's not stupid. But just . . . be prepared for stupid."

I wrinkled my nose at him. "Mal, I get why it's important for you to be the one to take Asher out, but if you're in trouble and I have a clear shot . . ."

"By all means, if I'm in trouble take the fucker out."

I laughed, expecting him to raise an argument. He leaned in to kiss me again; this time, his lips were more urgent. His heartbeat quickened and so did mine. There was no time. Mal's best chance to get close enough to the pack to draw them out was at dusk. He'd still have enough light to see well, but his own black coat would help camouflage him.

"Mal," I said when he finally broke away. "Promise me you'll come back to me. Even if it means it's just the two of us. I know Wild Lake's your home, but we could make our home anywhere."

He caressed my jaw with his thumb, and his amber eyes blazed gold. "Trust me, my love. And make sure you shoot straight."

He gave me another quick kiss that took my breath away, then he leaped down from the tree. He'd already shifted to his wolf as he hit the ground and took off like a bolt of lightning covered in black fur.

And then, I was alone, high in the air with the howling wind and swaying trees.

Chapter Twenty-Two

TIME SEEMED TO STOP, blend together and twist. Only my heartbeat marked the seconds. Mine and Mal's. We hadn't had a chance to discuss the ramifications, but that second marking, with me bent over the seat of the Range Rover, had changed me the deepest yet. I felt Mal's pulse, yes. But he transmitted something else. A rumbling rage moved through me. My breath quickened as his pace did. My muscles bunched as it felt like I took each step with him.

I could see a flash of green as trees and foliage whipped by Mal's field of vision. I could still see my own surroundings, but they were blended with Mal's if I reached out for him. It meant I might be able to feel what he felt. Exhilarating, exciting, terrifying. If Mal was wounded, it would rip through me too. Would my heart stop if his did? Maybe not physically, but I knew it would hurt me just the same. And I knew he could feel what I felt. I took a deep breath and let it out slow. If I panicked, if I was distracted, it could put him at greater risk. No. I could never do that. He needed me as much as I needed him.

It didn't take long. Mal's vision clouded red as bloodlust overtook him. Hunt. Kill. Win.

A howl rent the air, making every hair on my body stand on end. Mal. My Mal. I strained against the safety harness. When my Alpha called, every cell in me wanted to go to him. But, he was calling for someone else now. He stood stock still in the center of a clearing. His heart rate, despite the adrenalin coursing through him, stayed slow and steady.

Movement. A whiff of blood. Light flashed through the trees. No. Not here. There. I squeezed my eyes shut and opened them again. I had to stay present in my own surroundings. Mal would die if I didn't. I had to find a way to control the changes in me so I could focus on what he put me here to do.

Then Mal was on the move again. I felt his need to turn and fight. Running, fleeing was not in his nature. But this time, it was crucial. And he was right. He'd been right about everything. I felt hot breath, teeth snapping, coming close enough to scrape along his left flank.

"Mal," I whispered to myself. "Don't let them get so close."

I tried to close my mind. Mal needed every sense, every motion he took focused on a single point. Anything I did to interfere could be deadly.

Then I saw him. He was a streak of black fur and murderous rage. I raised the dart gun and sighted the scope. Mal stopped running. He stopped no more than twenty yards from the base of my tree. He threw his head back and howled, transmitting his position to every living thing within miles. But it was only one being that mattered.

Two gray wolves broke into the clearing together. I sighted the largest one. My aim was sure. I let out a breath and squeezed the trigger. I went out of my body. The dart hit the bigger gray wolf just behind his left shoulder. I didn't have time to see if it did any damage. I racked another round and aimed for the other wolf. He dove behind a tree but seemed disoriented, exposing his rump to me. Mal howled again and I got off another shot. This one went wild and stuck in the tree right next to the wolf.

"Fuck, fuck, fuck!"

I felt Mal presence inside me. Calm. Slow. Deliberate. I squeezed my eyes shut and racked another round. I had four darts left.

The first gray wolf lay quiet, slumped against a fallen log. If Luke were still out of commission, that left Asher and two more wolves against Mal. The other gray wolf rounded on Mal, but I was ready for it. I squeezed off another shot. This one stabbed right between the wolf's shoulder blades and he went down almost instantly.

God! It was working!

I loaded another dart and brought the gun up, looking for another target. I didn't have long to wait. My heart stuck in my throat as Asher emerged through the trees. His gold eyes blazed. His unmistakable red coat gleamed under the setting sun, making him nearly glow.

Mal was surrounded. Asher stood before him. Another large, gray wolf closed in from behind him. Then Luke stalked slowly through the trees and took a point at Mal's side looking strong and lethal. Blood poured out of the wound at Luke's shoulder, but it didn't seem to matter. I knew on instinct it was Asher who controlled him.

But, I could stop it. Sweat poured down my neck. My palms

grew sticky. I rubbed my right hand against my pant leg and braced the stock against my shoulder. I had Asher in my sights and that was all that mattered. Mal crouched low, getting ready to strike. I knew what would happen the instant he did. The three wolves would tear him to pieces. Asher would probably die too, but it wouldn't matter. Not to me.

I could kill Asher myself. The shotgun lay at my feet. But, at this range, the risk I might hit Mal was too great. At least with the darts, his life wasn't in danger. I squeezed the trigger.

Nothing happened. The gun was jammed.

The other gray wolf lunged for Mal, tearing a chunk of flesh from his back, right leg. Pain tore through my own leg but Mal didn't even flinch. He kept his eyes locked with Asher as they circled each other.

I put the dart gun down and grabbed the shotgun. I closed my eyes for an instant and tried to talk to Mal.

Back up. You're too close. I can't get a clear shot.

But, Mal had shut me out. The beast within him was in full control.

Luke lunged forward and I could see the strength leach out of him. He faltered, and swaying to the side he fell to the ground. It left an opening. Small, but enough. Mal stepped to the side and I was ready. I had Asher in my crosshairs.

I let out a breath and squeezed the trigger.

The shot cracked through the air followed almost immediately by a second one. The muscles in my arm quit on me, like someone had cut invisible puppet strings. My arms and legs twitched involuntarily and a blanket of blackness closed in on me.

Mal felt whatever hit me and turned away from Asher.

I had just enough strength to turn my head. Asher was at Mal's throat, his fangs dripping as he brought Mal down. God, had I missed? Had I fucking missed Asher? The other gray wolf closed in as well. And through the trees, I saw the long, cold barrel of another gun aimed straight at me as Byron Flood stepped into the clearing, and everything went dark.

Chapter Twenty-Three

"PRINCESS? BABY? COME ON BACK."

Sound seemed to have physical form and stabbed me right between the eyes. I wanted quiet, sleep, darkness. Rough hands on my shoulders shook me hard and wouldn't let me be.

A splash of cold water on my face and I was done for. Sputtering, I opened my eyes to see two blazing gold ones staring back at me.

"Fuck." It was all I could manage to say past a dry throat. Mal lifted me, bringing a cool cup of water to my lips and helping me drink.

"That's my girl," he said, pulling me close to his chest. He kissed my forehead.

"What happened?"

Mal smiled but it didn't quite reach his eyes. Deep lines of worry framed his face and sweat beaded his brow.

"You happened." An oddly familiar voice was at my side. I

turned my head. Luke sat next to me, his arm in a sling. He looked like hell. Maybe worse than I felt. But, he was human. He was whole. His wavy brown hair hung over the side of his face, but he'd trimmed the caveman beard. He leaned forward and put a hand on my shoulder.

"Luke?"

His green eyes flashed. A haunted, hollow look rimmed them, but the agony I'd seen in him before seemed to have melted away. I raised my head and looked around the dim room. We were back in Mal's cabin. I lay stretched out on the bed in Mal's arms. My legs felt swollen and fat. My right arm did too. I was naked, covered only by the thin cotton sheet Mal wrapped around me. I saw an angry red welt on my right upper arm.

"Flood got you with the other tranquilizer gun," Mal explained. "Thank Christ you had the shotgun instead of him or you'd probably be dead. That's going to smart for a few days, but I think you should probably have feeling in your arms and legs in a couple of hours."

"Flood?"

"Don't worry." A deep booming voice penetrated the room. With Mal's help, I got up to a fully seated position. The voice belonged to a stocky, clean-shaven hulk of a man standing in the doorway. A figure lay slumped at his feet, hog tied with thick cords of rope.

"Meet Dax," Mal whispered against my ear.

Dax ran a hand over his bald head and he kicked the figure on the floor, rolling him over so I could see his face. His was red, puffy, with both eyes swollen shut, but it was Professor Flood. He moaned and spat blood on the ground.

"He'll be all right," Dax said. He leaned against the door frame and casually sipped out of a tin cup. Coffee. Strong brewed. My stomach growled.

Dax moved away from the door as it swung open, flooding the cabin with light that seared my eyes. I could see the sun rising high over the trees. It was early morning. Two more hulking men stepped into the cabin. They looked so similar, I guessed they were brothers. Related at least for sure. They each had dark blond hair and gray eyes. They were broad-shouldered and burly, but they smiled warmly when they stepped in and saw me.

"That'd be Joe and Sam," Mal said. Joe, I guess it was, limped a little when he walked and recognition clicked. He was the one I hit with the dart gun myself. That he was up and walking while I was still laid flat underscored the extent of his werewolf strength.

"Good morning, ma'am," Joe said, looking sheepish and endearing.

"It's over then?" I looked up at Mal. "We did it? Asher's gone?"

Mal smiled but his eyes still had dark shadows in them. "His hold over the pack is broken. As you can see for yourself."

I may not have known Mal long, but he was in me. I knew when he was holding something back. "Where is he, Mal?"

Mal shrugged. "He's dead, baby. Just before Flood hit you, you hit Asher. I thought it was over. Hell, when I felt you go down, I *wanted* it to be over. Asher had me by the throat. But, then the juice kicked in and he faltered. The second he lost consciousness, the pack was free. It was pretty much a melee after that. I felt Flood's shot go into you and I had to get to you. It was more important than finishing Asher off. I thought . . . it sounded like a shotgun. I saw you slump over and it damn near finished me."

"But, he's dead. You said he's dead."

Mal gave me a solemn nod and looked over his shoulder. Luke sat at the hearth, wringing his hands together. "You killed Asher," I said to Luke .

He looked up at me, his eyes still haunted by whatever demons he held at bay. But, he shook his head. "No," he answered. "That was Mal's kill."

A vision flashed behind my eyes. Maybe it was from before I completely lost consciousness. Maybe it was something I saw from my connection to Mal. But, I saw Asher lying helpless as Luke staggered toward him on two legs. He got to him. Fell forward. Then Mal, still in his wolf came to his shoulder. Luke stepped aside as Mal lunged and tore Asher's throat apart. I watched as Asher's yellow eyes went dim and the rest of the pack closed in around him. Then each of them formed a circle around Mal and shifted back to their wolves, dipped their heads.

The rest of the men shifted around me. Casting their eyes down, they all went outside. Dax grabbed Flood by the feet and dragged him over the threshold too. Then, Mal and I were alone.

"My God," he said. Mal looked down and cradled my head in his palms. "For a second there I thought I'd lost you."

Mal took a breath. Something had happened. Something big. My blood started to heat as Mal's did. His pulse quickened and I felt that familiar twinge as his mood seemed to bleed into mine. I sensed something different though. We weren't alone.

Dax stood to the north of the cabin scanning the tree line. I *felt* Luke standing off just to the side of him. He wasn't at peace yet. Something tore at him, a longing that broke my heart a little. And Joe and Sam. They moved as a unit toward the south side of the cabin. I felt Joe shift first. It was just a flash, nothing like the clarity with which I could see through Mal's eyes. But, there could be no denying I had some connection with these other men now too.

"What's happening?"

Mal smiled and kissed the top of my head. "The pack has accepted me as Alpha. I challenged their Alpha and won. I could have claimed the pack by right, but they chose me anyway. Now, they can sense me and follow my commands. And because you're my mate, they're kind of hard-wired to you too. Each of them would lay down their lives for you."

Warmth flooded me as Mal held me. It felt good and right. A missing piece of Mal seemed to fill, one I hadn't realized until now he needed. He was safe and whole and all mine. Whatever else happened didn't matter as long as Mal was with me and the pack was here.

"What about Flood?" I asked.

Mal let out a chuckle that sent a shiver of warmth through me. "Him? Yeah. Dax is maybe getting a little carried away." No sooner had he said it then a yelp cut through the air. I couldn't see it, but I sensed Dax had hauled Flood to his feet only to watch him crumple to the ground again.

"As soon as you feel up to it, we're going to drop him off at the ranger station on the way out. It seems your professor has some things he'd like to say about what really happened back at the outpost. You might say he's had some clarity and a change of heart. See, Dax is very persuasive."

I couldn't help but laugh. My affection for Dax had already started to grow. With it, feeling started to flood back into my legs. I looked down and wiggled my toes.

"I think I'm starting to feel a lot better."

"Good," Mal said. "The pack is antsy to get on the move."

I could feel that too. Anticipation moved through the pack like an electrical current. "We need to get them home," I said, as their feeling of longing became mine. "How far is Wild Lake?"

Mal slid off the bed and held his hands out to me. I rose on unsteady legs as he wrapped the bed sheet around me and tucked it tight so it wouldn't fall. Then, I took the first slow steps toward the front door and sunlight. Mal kept me steady as we came to the doorway, ready to tell the others we were ready to take them home.

Chapter Twenty-Four

MY FIRST VIEW of Wild Lake was the bobbing tree tops as the Range Rover jostled up a dirt path. I lay with my head in Mal's lap, having slept most of the way through northern Michigan. The farther we went, the wilder the woods became around us. Maybe, in some faraway time in my life, that would have seemed unnatural. As if I were leaving everything I knew behind. Now though, with Mal at my side, it felt like a homecoming.

He gazed down at me, warmth flooding his eyes as the noon sunlight stabbed through the window. I lifted my hand to shield it from the brightness. Mal was at peace, but a new energy coursed through his veins. It was hard not to get swept up in it. Dax drove this final leg of the trip. Luke sat in the passenger seat and Mal and I were in back. Joe and Sam followed behind on a matching pair of Harleys. Soon, the pack would need to shift. I felt their urge to hunt, to explore the lands they called home. But, they had healing to do. We'd driven for several hours. Plenty of time for Dax to fill us in on the highlights of what they'd been through.

Asher had taken the pack out of their sanctuary in Kentucky. They had a home deep in the forests surrounding Mammoth Caves. I'd never been there, but my new connection to the pack filled in some of the gaps. The caves were cold and dark, stretching for miles in directions that had been unexplored by normal men.

After Asher's last skirmish with the Wild Lake packs, he started to go mad with his all-consuming lust for revenge. Nothing else mattered to him. Not the health of the pack or his own. When Luke and the others tried to reason with him he forced them all to shift, trapping them in the animal rage that ate away at him like a cancer.

Luke had suffered the worst because he was the closest to Asher and fought back the hardest. He kept himself distant, closed off a little from Mal and the rest of us. It would take time for him to heal. Mal felt confident Wild Lake itself would help bring him back the rest of the way.

I wasn't so sure. I watched Luke. He separated himself from the pack more than the others. His tortured gaze drifted to some far off place and agony that no one but he could ever truly understand. I hoped Mal was right. Luke was a good man. I could feel it. Whatever evil had touched his soul could never take that away from him.

"This is as far as we can drive," Dax finally said, jamming the Rover into park and shutting off the engine. He threw the door open and stretched his limbs. Mal and I followed suit. Excitement crackled through the pack. Joe and Sam came to stand at Dax's side with Mal leading the way. He held my hand as we started down a rocky path leading to a large yellow and white farm house perched high on a hill.

The place looked straight out of a picture postcard with a

wrap-around porch, white picket fence, and long porch swing at the front. A light mist hung near the tips of the tall pines surrounding the house. A large, rustic, red barn with white trim stood behind the house. Beyond that, Mal told me was Wild Lake itself. Nearly four hundred acres of pristine waters surrounded by lush, green forests, he told me.

Mal cupped his hands to his mouth and whistled. The shrill ring of it pierced my ears. The front screen door flew open and I could make out two figures standing on the porch. A man and a woman. Older. It was hard to tell from the distance, but I guessed in their seventies. The woman walked slowly down the porch steps. She had thick, wild, wavy gray hair that flowed behind her as she quickened her step. She was short and round, and her bare white legs poked out from under a bright green housecoat. Halfway across the yard she froze.

The old man behind her held on to the porch railing. He looked at us but didn't focus on anything in particular. Even so, I could see the corners of his mouth lift into a smile.

The woman began to flap her hands. Barefoot, she broke into a run toward us, screaming wildly. She moved fast for someone her size and age. "Heaven's sake! Oh, Jesus! Malcolm!"

She stopped right in front of us, breathless. She had a warm, kind face with bright green eyes that flashed in a way that seemed familiar. But, instinctively, I knew she was human, just like me.

"Laura," Mal stepped forward. "This is Pat. Up there's Harold. Wild Lake belongs to them."

Pat flapped a hand. "Oh, bullshit, Malcolm. Our name's on the paperwork, but you know this is your home." She emphasized the word home and her smile brightened. She lunged forward and pulled Mal into a rib-crushing hug. He smiled and lifted her effortlessly off her feet, giving the old woman a twirl and a thrill that brought laughter bubbling up out of me.

When he set her down, she turned to me, smiling wide. She stepped forward and put her hands on my cheeks. She was warm and kind, smelling of baked goods and wood soap. I liked her immediately.

"Who have you brought?"

"Princess Laura," Mal teased.

"Prince," I said. "My name is Laura Prince."

"Not for long." Mal's voice was deep, dark, and filled with mischief. He shot me a look that sent a thrill of heat tickling along my spine. Pat didn't miss it. She put a hand on her hip and another around my shoulders. She reached back and felt the mark at the base of my neck and gave me a knowing smile.

"Well, welcome home Laura. Don't let these dogs give you too much trouble. You probably haven't had access to warm running water and home cooking since you threw in with these boys. You let me take care of you while you're here." My shoulders sagged with relief at her invitation. I hadn't realized how much I missed hot baths.

She wrapped her arm around me and steered me toward the house. "I've got a room ready you can claim. Clean clothes too. I've learned to be prepared when the boys come home."

"I don't even know how to begin to thank you."

Pat clucked as she led me down the hill. We would have kept on going, but Mal called out to us.

"Pat," Mal said, his voice taking on a solemn tone. "There's something else."

Pat stiffened next to me and her arm fell off my shoulder. She trembled and I had the urge to go to her, offer her a steadying hand. But, she put up a palm to stop me. The old man had made his way down from the porch. He took halting steps and held a cane out in front of him. I saw immediately why. He had an old but deep scar slashing across his face, rendering his cloudy blue eyes sightless. Claw marks. A shudder ran through me as I guessed exactly what type of creature could have made them.

Pat drew her shoulders back and turned to face Mal. Her eyes filled with dread as she seemed to brace herself for whatever news Mal needed to share. The car door opened and closed behind me and Luke walked slowly toward us. In all the excitement, I hadn't noticed he'd hung back until now. Pat's hands flew to her mouth and tears sprang from her eyes. Mal moved quicker than I did. He got behind her and held her up by the elbows before she would have fallen to the ground.

She reached out a shaky hand as tears streamed down her face. Luke's eyes misted as well as he came to her. It was the first sign of emotion I'd seen in Luke since I'd met him. Pat reached out and touched his face, tracing the lines of Luke's jaw as if she were the one who was blind.

"Hi Mama," Luke said. "I'm home."

Mama. Of course Pat's eyes seemed familiar. They were a match for her son's. I choked past a lump in my throat as Pat let out a sob and folded her son against her breast. The old man came beside him and put a hand on Luke's shoulder. He was crying too.

"Good to have you back," he said.

"Good to be back, Uncle Harold," Luke said quietly.

Mal clasped his hand in mine and gestured with his chin to the rest of the pack. Whatever passed between them, Luke, Pat, and Harold deserved to have this moment in private.

LATER, when the sun set, Mal took me to Wild Lake. Since he'd been made Alpha, the pack had been with us constantly. Though I relished the time I got to spend getting to know them, I missed my time with Mal. Now, a full moon rose high and I sat resting my head against his chest on a large outcropping of rock overlooking the lake. The water was still as glass, mirroring the starlit sky and wooded horizon so it was hard to tell where one began and the other ended.

"I love it here," I said, leaning the back of my head against his chest. After her reunion with Luke, Pat made me feel like it was my home too. She'd made me a huge pot of chicken noodle soup while the pack took to the woods to hunt. They needed their time together and I felt the bond among them . . . among all of us strengthen as we breathed in the pure air of Wild Lake.

"I'm glad. You know, I'll go anywhere in the world with you, Laura, but this place is special. I was hoping you'd love it as much as I do."

"Oh. I do. How could I not? I can't explain it. But, it almost feels like the land is part of the pack too.

I snuggled against him. With the lake to ourselves, we'd stripped naked. Mal's growing erection pressed against the small of my back as I threaded my fingers through his. Moisture pooled between my legs as my own urgent need rose. We'd have another moment or two, but soon I wouldn't be able to stand not having him inside me.

"I'm glad," he said. "I've talked to Harold and Pat and a few of the other Alphas who call Wild Lake home. We can stay here. I've been given a claim further north. We can build a home there if you'd like. I can take back my piece of the business."

"What business?"

"Wild Lake Outfitters."

I tilted my head back to look at him. "Wild Lake Outfitters. That's you?" I knew the name. Even as far west as Green Bluff, my father only bought W.L.O. hunting and fishing gear. I hadn't put two and two together until now.

Mal nodded. "I've got a stake in it, yeah. All of the Wild Lake packs do. You didn't think we lived on venison and rabbit alone, did you?"

I laughed. My Alpha was full of surprises. Ones I hoped I'd have a lifetime to unravel.

"My home is wherever you are." I said it and I meant it, but even so, I felt unsettled.

"What is it?" Mal asked. Of course he sensed my moods just as I did his.

I shifted in his arms and tilted my head again to meet his eyes. "It's just, I still want to finish what I started. Flood's confessed, so my scholarship and my standing at G.L.U. has been restored. I'm three semesters away from graduating and they've offered me a spot in their graduate program. Flood's going to jail for what he did, so I don't have to worry about him anymore."

Mal stiffened. He reached down and smoothed a lock of hair

away from my face. "I don't want you to worry about anyone like Flood ever hurting you again."

I leaned up to kiss him. "I'm not. But, I think the last few weeks have given me a taste of what pack life can be like, Mal. We've earned some peace, but the packs still have enemies, don't they?"

His silence was all the answer I needed.

"I said I want to finish what I started. I want to learn all I can about what makes you were. What happens during the Rise and what happens after that. Why there aren't as many female werewolves. I want to understand the science of it. So if there *is* some kind of biological threat to you, to us, maybe we can fight that too. So yes. I'm going to finish my degree at G.L.U. They have a global campus. If there's internet in these northern lands of which you speak, hook me up and let's rock and roll. And then we can . . ."

Mal quieted me with hot kisses. He lifted me and turned me so I laid flat on my back on the smooth rock, my legs spread beneath him. I giggled as my hair fanned out and spilled over the side of the rock.

He took each of my ankles in his hand and spread them, making a wide V with my legs. I gasped as he slid his hard cock into me, sheathing himself to the root.

"I love your mind as much as your body, my princess. You want to be a werewolf vet when you grow up?" He bit his bottom lip and closed his eyes, savoring the pleasure of my warm, wet pussy as he thrust in and out of me.

I moaned and arched my back, basking in the pleasure of him as well. "M-maybe." Though it was getting harder and harder to form a rational thought.

Mal's eyes snapped open as he reached the deepest parts of me. He let go of my ankles as I wrapped them around his shoulders. From this angle, Mal was inside me as far as he could go.

"But, I can tell you what happens after the Rise, my love." He reached around and his fingers traced the outlines of the crescent shaped scar on my neck. His mark. His brand. As always, it pulsed to match the growing need between my legs. Two perfect points of pleasure, forever connecting me to Mal. He leaned down and nipped at my ear.

"Tell me," I gasped.

"The Heat." He growled his answer and a new dark desire rose within me.

"Heat? You can put me in heat? You mean there's a level higher than what I'm feeling right now. My God Mal, I can't get enough of you as it is. I think if you put me in heat, I might as well just stay right here on this rock and keep you inside of me forever."

His laughter was low, wicked, and filled with lust. "Not a half bad idea, my love. But, lucky for the both of us, it can take a long time to bring a human woman into heat. It could take years. And we'll have to keep practicing."

I gasped as he increased the rhythm of his thrusting. The moon shadowed him in white and blue and I could see the stars reflected in his eyes. A perfect symbol of what Mal was for me and I to him. He was my world, my moon and my stars. Whatever happened, whatever we did, we'd do it together.

"Practicing?" My words were breathless as the first edges of my orgasm made my legs quiver.

"Mmm hmm. Just like this." He rattled my teeth with another powerful thrust.

"Oh, God. Yes. I think I want that. Mmmm."

"Good. Because it's all I want too, Laura." His tone grew serious and he froze, impaling me with his turgid, throbbing cock. It took everything in me to still myself and look into his eyes.

"I want you, Laura. All of you. Your body. Your mind. Your soul. You already have mine. Until I found you, I never realized how alone I was. You've given me my life back, not just my pack. And, I'll spend the rest of my life making you happy. Whether it's here at Wild Lake or wherever you want to go."

I leaned up and kissed him. "I want that too, Mal. I meant it. I'm yours."

He smiled and clasped my bottom lip between his teeth, sending a new shock of heat through me.

He brought himself up on his elbows and smiled down at me. "Good. Then say it." He thrust slowly into me again, torturing me. I ground my hips against him, wanting him to increase the pace.

"I'm yours."

His body shook with that low, sultry laugh again as he moved inside me. "Prove it."

I snapped my eyes open and dug my nails into his back until his eyes flashed wild. "You're in me. How else can I prove it?"

He smiled and kissed me again. "Marry me, Laura." He thrust into me again, torturously slow. "Say it."

He held himself still, making me squirm. Heat grew inside me.

My juices poured out of me, coating us both. "Yes!" I gasped. And I meant it. I knew with perfect clarity at that moment that I was born for Mal and he for me. We were fated. I would be his mate, his lover, his wife, his partner, his princess. I saw his love for me in the flash of his golden eyes.

"Again." He thrust inside me.

I bucked beneath him, overcome by the grips of my passion. "Yes!" I cried, branding him in my own way with my nails down his back. "Oh, yes!"

Then, Mal finally lost control and gave into the wild lust raging inside. We came together as he threw his head back and let out a growl. The wolf was tamed for now, but not for long. And I relished it. Mal. The wolf. The pack. The moon and the lake surrounding us. I belonged to all of it. He belonged to me. As Mal poured his seed inside me I screamed my answer again and again.

Yes. It was always yes. My Alpha. My life. My love.

The End

A Note from Kimber White

I hope you enjoyed Mal and Laura's story as much as I enjoyed writing it. This one truly kept me up at night. It still does! And this was just the beginning of the stories from Wild Lake that I can't wait to bring you. Luke's story is up next. He's just starting to deal with the ramifications of having Asher in his head for so long. If he wants his happy ending, Luke's going to have to learn to control the beast inside of him. I have it on good authority there's a kickass beauty willing to help him out with that. Luke's story is told in <u>Dark Wolf</u>.

Keep Reading for a Bonus Book Right Now!

As my special gift to you, I've included the first installment of the prequel to *Rogue Alpha*. We first met some of the Wild Lake Wolves in my series *Claimed by the Pack*. If you haven't read it and would like to know more about what happened to Mal before he came to Manistee and met Laura, check out *The Alpha's Mark*. It's the first book in that series and I'm giving it to you at the end of this note as a limited time bonus. So keep reading!

A Note from Kimber White

For an exclusive first look at my next new release, sign up for my newsletter today. You'll be the first to know about my new releases and special discounts available only to subscribers. You'll also get a FREE EBOOK right now, as a special welcome gift for joining. I promise not to spam you, share your email or engage in other general assholery. You can unsubscribe anytime you like (I'll only cry a little). You can sign up here! http://www.kimberwhite.com/wild-lake-wolves/wild-lake-wolves-news

Psst . . . can I ask you a favor?

If you liked this story, can you do something for me? Please leave a review wherever you purchased it. Reviews help authors like me stay visible and allow me to keep bringing you more stories.

And if you STILL want more, I'd love to hang out with you on Facebook. I like to share story ideas, casting pics, and general insanity on a daily basis.

From the bottom of my heart though, THANK YOU for your support. You rock hard.

See you on the wild side!

Kimber

KimberWhite.com

kimberwhiteauthor@gmail.com

Special Bonus Excerpt - The Alpha's Mark

The Alpha's Mark

By
Kimber White

Copyright © 2015 by Kimber White

All Rights Reserved

No part of this book may be reproduced or transmitted in any form or by any means, electronic or mechanical including photocopying, recording, or by any information storage and retrieval system, without the written permission of the author or publisher, except where permitted by law or for the use of brief quotations in a book review.

This is a work of fiction. Names, characters, businesses, places, events, and incidents are either the products of the author's imagination or used in a fictitious manner. Any resemblance to actual persons, living or dead, or actual events is purely coincidental.

One - The Alpha's Mark

In just over ten miles of freeway, it seemed I'd gone from civilization to vast wilderness. This stretch of I-94 East took me through hilly terrain and forest on both sides. The towering pines and thick maples should have put me at ease. I should have enjoyed the sharp, musky scent of the woods and the open sky as dusk settled in. But, this was a foreign land to me, and I was hundreds of miles from the only home I'd ever known, with no plans to ever go back. This wasn't my place. I was just passing through. Part of me resented the cool, crisp wilderness air traced with a hint of ozone. A storm brewed from the North.

The first dusting of sprinkling rain hit the windshield of my Ford Escape. I fiddled with the instruments to set the wipers. A breeze picked up, and the tops of the tallest trees on either side of the road started to sway. A crack of thunder made me jump in my seat. A jagged streak of lightning speared into the woods far to the east, and a faint puff of smoke curled up above the tree line.

One - The Alpha's Mark

I worked the radio dial, trying to find something local for news of a tornado. I tried to remember, is it safer to stay with your car or find a ditch if you're caught in one? Rain pelted down in earnest. The storm had come up so fast. A leaf plastered to my windshield and got stuck under the wiper blades. Each swipe left a thick smear across my field of vision, and I adjusted the blade speed, trying to loosen it.

I ducked down, trying to find a spare patch of clear windshield. The rain angled right toward me in thick, heavy drops. If it got much worse, I was going to have to pull over. I did not want to be stuck out here. This wasn't me. This wasn't my place. I had no place anymore.

I didn't know how much further I had to go until I reached Ann Arbor. Four hours? Maybe less, if this storm didn't hold me up. I just wanted to get there, except I didn't really want to *be* there. Two years ago, it would have been my dream. I earned a music scholarship in voice to the University of Michigan. My Dad had been so proud of me. It would make me the first person in our family to graduate from college. I was all set to leave, and Dad got sick.

Though he'd never smoked a day in his life, he contracted an aggressive form of lung cancer. They said it was probably caused by his years as a fireman. He fought hard, and lasted longer than most with his same diagnosis. He hung on for over a year. But then just after Christmas, he finally let go. I'd forgone college to take care of him. It was just the two of us. He had no one else. College could wait. But now, seven months later, I'd lost him, and it was time for me to start my own life. Everyone said so.

Another crack of thunder, and a flash of lightning came even closer. I jumped in my seat again as I struggled to see out of

One - The Alpha's Mark

my hopelessly smeared window. A tree limb slammed down in front of me. I swerved to the left to get around it, and almost ended up in a ditch. My heart tripped and my fingers trembled as I gripped the steering wheel. That was a close one.

The leaf dislodged from my windshield, and I could finally see again. I straightened the wheel, and veered the Escape back across the median. I crested the top of a large hill and started to coast back down, letting my foot up off the accelerator.

Two golden eyes seemed to appear out of thin air at the bottom of the hill. I blinked hard, trying to let my brain catch up. A wolf stood in the middle of the road directly in my path. It stood still and calm, with its great brown head slightly cocked to the side and its ears perked straight up, as if it were deciding what to make of me.

Why didn't it move? I punched the horn, but the wolf didn't so much as blink its shining, golden eyes. I slammed on the brakes. There was no way I wouldn't hit the thing. The back of the car fishtailed, and I lost control of it. I tried to wrench the steering wheel hard right.

The wolf stood there. Just before the moment of impact, I swore I saw it dip its head, almost as if it were acknowledging its fate. The world became a sickening crunch of metal on bone and flesh. Blood, mixed with rain, sprayed my windshield as the car careened into the ditch just past the shoulder of the road.

My world was a cloud of white and the taste of metal as my airbag deployed and blood filled my mouth. I might have blacked out. What had been noise, chaos, and panic became calm and quiet, except for the steady rhythm of the pelting rain.

One - The Alpha's Mark

I don't know how long I sat there. It was at least a moment or two. Maybe more. I finally reached over and unlatched my seat belt. My right shoulder blossomed in pain. I wiggled my fingers and toes. I pushed the airbag down and pulled down the visor mirror. A small line of blood trickled out of my nose and my lip was split, but I seemed to be more or less whole.

The car door protested with a creak when I pushed it open. The Escape had landed on an angle, resting mostly on the passenger side, so I had to crawl up and out. I had the presence of mind to grab my backpack. I made it two steps up toward the shoulder of the road when my phone buzzed to life.

"911. What is your emergency?" said a female voice.

My fingers shook as I slid the screen open. The car was equipped with 911 Assist. My father had insisted on it. The minute the airbag deployed, the car's computer sent the call through.

"I've crashed," I said. I wiped the blood and rain out of my face as I pressed the phone to my ear.

"Are you injured, ma'am?" the dispatcher said.

"I don't think so. I'm a little banged up but I've gotten out of the car. I'm not sure where I am, though."

"We'll be able to find you," she said. "But it will go a lot faster if you can help me out."

I looked around. When the rain started, I hadn't thought to pay attention to any mile markers.

"I just crossed over into Michigan from South Bend. I think Kalamazoo is the next biggest city. I haven't seen another car in miles, though. It's really wooded here."

One - The Alpha's Mark

"Okay, I think I've got you, more or less. We're sending someone to you," the dispatcher said. "Can you stay with your vehicle?"

"Yeah," I said. My head started to throb and I felt a little woozy. Maybe I had hit it harder than I thought. "Yeah. Can you tell them to hurry, though? It's getting dark out here, and I think there are wolves in the area. I hit one."

"Wolves? Did you say wolves? Probably not, ma'am. You probably saw a coyote."

The call started to break up. I climbed out of the ditch and stood on the gravel shoulder. I looked to my left and right. I was completely alone out here, with the woods all around me. Icy fingers of panic started to snake their way through my belly, and I concentrated on breathing.

My phone gave one last dying beep, and the 911 operator was gone for good. It was okay, though. Help was on the way. I'd given them plenty of information to find me.

Mercifully, the rain let up as I stepped up to the road. There had to be a town no more than ten or fifteen miles to the east. Had to be. They ought to be able to get someone out here in fifteen minutes or less.

I became aware of a keening cry to my left. It was the sound of an animal in pain, and probably dying. I don't know what compelled me to walk toward it, but I did.

She lay on her left side, her shoulders heaving with the effort of breathing. It *was* a she. Somehow, I knew this even before I got to her. This was ludicrous. Insanity. Never mind it was growing dark as I stood in the middle of an Interstate highway. Never mind this was a wild animal fighting to live. But, I went to her.

One - The Alpha's Mark

Something in me pulled me to her, and I crouched in front of her.

She panted from the strain of her last breaths, and she craned her neck backward to get a look at me. I meant to keep a few feet of distance between us, but when her haunting golden eyes met mine, I reached out and laid my hand on the top of her head. Her thick, brown fur was coarse and lush under my fingertips. I smoothed it back, rubbing behind her ears. She laid them flat, her gaze flicking over me, taking me in.

"I'm so sorry," I heard myself say. "It's almost over."

And it was. With each gasping breath this magnificent creature took, life slowly drained away. I could *feel* it. Her eyes dimmed though she kept them locked on mine. She seemed to need me. My presence calmed her as I smoothed my hand over her head with a slow, soothing rhythm.

"It's okay," I said. "You can let go now. No one can hurt you anymore."

She whined and let out a chuff through her moist, black nose, then curled her lips back, panting. She nuzzled her head against my hand as her eyelids fluttered. She had thick, black lashes. There was something so intelligent about her eyes. She *knew* who I was. It was like she could understand what I was saying.

"I'll stay with you," I said. "It won't be long now." Tears welled behind my own eyes and a lump knotted in my throat. "You can rest. It's all right. You can be finished." My voice quivered. God, I'd said those same words. I'd held his hand until he took his last breath and his clear eyes went dark.

This great, beautiful wolf's chest rose and fell for the last time as I held her head in my hands. "Goodbye, great lady," I said.

One - The Alpha's Mark

She opened her eyes one last time. They narrowed, with what I could swear was understanding. And there was something else as well. As her pulse slowed under my touch and finally ceased, she seemed at peace. She lifted her chin one last time and closed her eyes. Then she died in my arms.

Two - The Alpha's Mark

I don't know how long I crouched there—a few minutes maybe. I couldn't leave her. After the wolf died, I tried to pull her toward the side of the road. My own sense of self-preservation had finally started to return. A car could come barreling down on us at any moment. I couldn't bear to watch her poor body crushed a second time.

I couldn't move her even an inch, though. She was far too heavy. I gave one last effort, pain exploding in my shoulder as I tried to pull her by her front paws. Two things made me stop short.

First, a plaintive wail seemed to come from all sides. I jerked my head up and looked into the woods. I couldn't be sure, but I thought I saw a flash of yellow eyes. They were gone almost as soon as they appeared.

Then, headlights flooded the ground in front of me and I rose to my feet. I waved my stiff arms in the air as the siren drowned out any noises from the forest. I wanted to warn the driver off from striking the dead wolf, and to help me. The

Two - The Alpha's Mark

patrol car crested the hill and came to stop by the side of the road, just behind my wrecked vehicle.

I hated to leave the wolf lying there in the middle of the road. She was dead, I knew, but I still didn't want to leave her side. The officer stepped out of his vehicle. It was a white sedan with gold lettering, its red and blue lights nearly blinding me as they flashed, though he'd turned off the wailing siren.

"You okay, ma'am?" The deputy tipped his brown hat, as he looked cautiously across the road. The rain had let up, and now it was nothing more than a slow drizzle.

"I'm okay," I said. "I'm afraid she's dead, though. I tried to stop, but I couldn't."

The deputy nodded. His face was kind and handsome. I saw a tuft of white-blond hair peeking out under his hat, and even from this distance noted his clear, blue eyes. He was young, maybe in his mid-twenties, just a few years older than me. "I'm going to need you to step over here, though, ma'am. Come back toward the vehicles, if you don't mind."

There was something odd about his tone, like he was handling me. I supposed I probably did look a little crazy, just then, as I tried to pull the wolf out of the middle of the road.

"Will you help me?" I asked. I still had a grip on the wolf's front paws. "We can't just leave her here."

"Ma'am." His voice took a hard edge. "You do need to leave her, okay? Just come on over here, and let's see about getting you taken care of. We're gonna have to let the DNR tend to her, all right? I'll call them just as soon as possible."

There was something about his voice and posture. He kept one hand on the butt of his service weapon, and his eyes scanned the tree line behind me. Cold fear crept through my spine, and

Two - The Alpha's Mark

I gently rested the wolf's paws back on the road and straightened my back. A low rumble filled the relative quiet. It reached my skin and my nerve endings before my ears. A chorus of menacing growls seemed to come from all directions.

My breath seemed to leave my lungs as I stepped away from the wolf and toward the deputy. He'd dropped into a half crouch and unhooked his service weapon from its holster. He motioned toward me with the flick of his hand as he watched the trees. Something had him spooked, and my skin prickled.

"We need to get you out of here," he said, his voice barely above a whisper, but filled with urgency.

"Okay," I said. I turned back toward the fallen wolf and wished I hadn't. Golden eyes seemed to float in the darkness behind the trees. One pair, two. Half a dozen.

"Just go ahead and get in the back seat."

It was a good idea. I didn't want to step around the patrol car toward the woods for anything. I slipped into the back seat as he got into the front. He didn't say a word as he slammed the car into gear and turned the wheel hard until we were facing east again, and his tires squealed as he slammed on the accelerator.

"What was that?" I said, afraid to look back.

The deputy straightened in his seat.

"Oh, don't worry. A storm like that can scare up all kinds of wildlife." he deflected. Gone was the alarm he'd shown just a few moments before. "You sure you're not hurt?"

"No," I said. "I've just got a little bit of a split lip where the airbag hit me. And I think I bit my tongue. My shoulder's sore, but I got off easy."

Two - The Alpha's Mark

I let the rest of my thought kind of hang there. I got off easy. The wolf didn't. I resisted the urge to look back at her one last time. She was so beautiful. There had been intelligence behind her eyes. Why in the world hadn't she moved out of the way?

"Well," the deputy said cheerfully, "let's go ahead and get you checked out, in any case. My station's just a few miles out. We can see about calling your insurance company and get you on your way."

I leaned back in my seat. Now that the excitement seemed to be passed, I started to feel drowsy, and that raised alarm bells in my head. Maybe I *had* hit my head harder than I thought. The deputy took the next exit, and soon we were headed down wooded dirt roads. I was soaked to the bone and started to shiver.

"What's your name?" he asked.

"Oh," I answered. "I probably should have started with that. It's Neve. Neve Dalton. I was on my way to U. of M."

He nodded, and looked at me through the rearview mirror. "Nice to meet you, Neve. We'll get you back on your way soon enough. Let's just fill out an accident report and make sure you're not in need of any medical attention."

"Thank you," I said. "How much longer exactly?" We seemed to be headed further and further away from civilization, and my hackles started to raise. Maybe I should have asked for I.D., but he was in a marked patrol car and in uniform.

"I'm not a county deputy," he answered as if he could sense my growing unease. "I mean, I'm deputized. But I'm a park ranger, technically. You can call me Jake. Jake Glanville."

"Huh," I said. "Park Ranger Jake. Why did the 911 dispatcher send you out?"

Two - The Alpha's Mark

He smiled. "I was just the closest to you. That's all. The storms knocked out a few power lines closer, so the county boys have their hands full taking calls."

He made another turn. It was just about full dark now. The patrol car's headlights shone on a large, wooden sign. "Hidden Forest Nature Reserve." Ranger Jake made a last slow turn and took us down a dirt road going deeper into the woods.

His tires crunched on the gravel as he took a long, winding driveway up to a cabin at the top of the hill. Two other patrol cars were parked in front of it as he came to a stop and stepped out of the car.

It was pitch black, and when Ranger Jake opened the passenger door to let me out, I found myself scanning the woods for more golden eyes in the darkness.

Jake looked down at me with kind eyes and a warm smile, and held his hand out. I shook off my skittishness and took it. Then I followed him into the log cabin outpost at the top of the hill.

I almost felt normal again as he opened the creaking screen door and jangled his keys until he found the right one. I was still freezing, and my wet clothes were plastered to my skin, but that wasn't what raised the hairs on the back of my neck and made me shiver. Somewhere, out in the darkness, I heard a single keening wail and knew in an instant what it was.

A wolf's howl. It was some distance away, but the sound of it curdled my blood. Maybe I really had hit my head harder than I thought, but the sound I heard was filled with grief and pain, but something else as well. It sounded like a warning.

Three - The Alpha's Mark

I stepped inside the cabin behind Ranger Jake, eager to get behind four walls and a lockable door. The cabin was large and mercifully warm. Jake flicked a light switch on the wall and the harsh fluorescents flared to life. The building was a long rectangle with state maps covering the pine-paneled walls, and several desks arranged around the room.

"Have a seat," Jake said. He lobbed his hat on one of the desks and ran a hand through his unruly blond hair. He really was young. Maybe closer to my twenty years than I first thought. He had the long, lanky build of a distance runner. Something about the way he carried himself set me on even more of an edge than my circumstances. Jake shot me an automatic smile whenever he caught my eye. The rest of the time, he looked back at the door, and chewed his bottom lip.

I took a seat at one of the desks and worked on getting circulation back to my hands and feet.

"Coffee sound good?" Jake called out as he stepped through

Three - The Alpha's Mark

another door at the back of the room. "Might be a little stale, but it'll be hot."

"Sounds perfect," I called out as Jake disappeared behind the door. As soon as he'd gone, I took the opportunity to scope out my surroundings a little more. The maps and posters on the wall detailed the wildlife native to the area. One poster showcased the frogs and turtles of Michigan in brilliant color. Another featured waterfowl. A third showed fish. Another poster highlighted the hundreds of large and small lakes dotted throughout Michigan.

I heard some kind of commotion behind the door where Jake disappeared. Another door slammed deeper in the building. A loud bang as something crashed to the floor. Jake finally reemerged bearing a steaming cup of coffee in a white Styrofoam cup. He smiled wide as he handed it to me. I didn't get much of a chance to enjoy it before the cabin door flew open. Jake's face lost all color.

Three of the largest men I'd ever seen charged in together. The biggest of the three slammed the door behind him loud enough to make the whole cabin shake beneath my feet. The two who came in before him had to be well over six feet, broad and thick like linebackers.

"Uh," Jake said. "Miss Dalton. Let's see about getting you started on that paperwork."

At least, I think that's what he said. I couldn't take my eyes off the last man towering in the doorway. He was so tall, he had to duck to come in through the door. His flinty gray eyes penetrated me, glowering with menace, raw power, and sex. His broad shoulders filled the door frame as the other two men flanked him. But I couldn't look at them. The big one held my gaze, daring me to look away. He worked the muscles of his

Three - The Alpha's Mark

anvil-sharp jaw, dusted with coarse black stubble. His beard couldn't hide his full, sensual mouth that seemed set in a permanent pout. He wore a white t-shirt that stretched across his rippled chest, his biceps straining against the sleeves. His waist tapered down into faded blue jeans that hugged his massive thighs.

"What the hell is this, Jake?" he said in a rich baritone that vibrated across my skin.

Jake stepped forward, his hands shaking as he handed me a pad of paper. "Just write down what happened," he said. "It'll make it easier when you deal with your adjuster." I took the paper, eager to focus on something other than that cruel, beautiful gaze from the mountain of a man still standing in the doorway.

"Let's talk outside," Jake said. A quick jerk of the larger man's chin was all it took to make Jake and the other two men fall into step behind him, and they walked outside. Alone now in the cabin, I shivered again, but this time it wasn't from the cold.

I wanted my car. I wanted to get the hell out of here. The only thing clear to me was that I had unwittingly walked into the middle of something between these men that seemed to have nothing and everything to do with me. They spoke in hushed voices that were still loud enough to carry through the thin walls, so I could pick out a few words and phrases.

"It was Magda," I heard Jake say. "She's dead, Tuck. I got there too late to do anything about it. I didn't see Ash, but you could be sure he was close."

Rumbling. I heard something smash against the side of the cabin. It might have been a fist or a boot.

Three - The Alpha's Mark

"Why the *hell* did you bring her here?" This came from the leader of the group. Tuck? For the rest of my life I'd remember the deep tone of his voice. It made me scared for Jake. Whatever the hell was going on between them, Jake had earned this man's ire, and I hoped I never would. The sooner I could get a hold of my insurance company and a rental car, the sooner I could get the hell out of here.

I didn't wait for Ranger Jake or any of the rest of them to come back. I pulled out my insurance card and called from the landline. I gave the representative the particulars of my situation. After a few minutes of repetitive questions, I got the answer I dreaded. Yes, I had rental car coverage. No, they wouldn't be able to send something out until tomorrow morning.

"You've got to be kidding me," I said to the rep. It wasn't her fault. Not really. She was probably reading most of what she told me from a script. "What do you expect me to do in the meantime?"

"Well," she said. "If you spend the night in a hotel, we can reimburse you up to one hundred dollars. And we'll send someone out tomorrow with the rental car. You're going to have to make arrangements to have the car towed to a body shop anyway. I'll give you a list of places in the area where you can take it."

"Great," I said, just as Jake and the others came back into the cabin. The insurance rep said more things, but my focus wasn't on her anymore. Mr. Tall, Dark, and Pissed Off charged back in and skewered me with eyes that flashed like fire. My heart tripped in my chest, and my mouth went dry. I didn't know who he was. I couldn't fathom why he looked so angry with me. But something happened when he came close. My skin

Three - The Alpha's Mark

prickled with gooseflesh and his presence seemed to warm me from the inside out.

I finished up with the insurance lady and hung up the phone.

"All set?" Jake said. He slapped his hands together and gave me that nervous smile.

"Not quite. They can't send a rental car out until the morning. It looks like I'm stuck here. Can you recommend a clean, cheap motel or something?"

The big guy let out a sound low in his throat just like a growl.

"May I help you?" I said. "I didn't ask for any of this. I don't want to be here anymore than it looks like you want me to be here."

He cocked his head to the side and a smirk came over his face. God. He was gorgeous, if not scary as hell. He jerked his chin again at the two burly men next to him. They looked similar enough to be brothers. Both had wavy, chestnut hair, broad noses, and wide set eyes. They stood at attention on either side of the room, and their eyes darted from me to this Tuck. They wore plain clothes, not uniforms—worn jeans and work boots. Faded t-shirts that showed off their hard muscles just like Tuck's did. They moved around their leader and headed toward the back of the cabin and the door Jake went through when he got my coffee.

"Jake," the leader said. "Why don't you drive Miss Dalton to the Woodland Inn off of 94?"

It unsettled me that he knew my name but hadn't bothered to introduce himself. Jake cleared his throat and plastered on that unhelpful smile.

Three - The Alpha's Mark

"Sure thing," he said. "It's clean. It's cheap. And they have better cell reception than we do."

"Perfect," I said. More than anything, I just wanted to get the hell out of this cabin, and away from the watchful eye of Jake's boss, or whoever he was. Though he wasn't in uniform, Jake clearly took orders from him.

"We'd better get a move on, then," Jake said. "There's another storm moving in, and the whole area's under a flood and tornado watch."

I pulled my purse and backpack off the desk and slung them over my shoulder. Jake grabbed his hat and held it in front of him as he waited for me by the door.

"I'm ready," I said. Jake held the door open. As I passed in front of the boss, Tuck, my skin prickled again. He stood just a few inches away from me. I swear I felt heat coming off of him. My fingers twitched and I had to resist the urge to put a hand on his rock hard chest as I came around him. I pursed my lips before I smiled up at him as I stepped through the front door after Jake.

Jake held the passenger door of his patrol car open for me. He straightened his hat on his head and closed the door after I stepped inside.

As Jake got in and backed the car away from the cabin, I couldn't help but look back. Jake's boss hadn't acknowledged me when we left. He didn't say goodbye, good luck, or anything. My first thought was to hope I'd never have to see him again. As soon as the words formed in my head though, something else stirred me to my core. The thought of *never* seeing him again left an ache in me that was completely unexpected.

Three - The Alpha's Mark

I saw two smoldering silver-gray eyes stare back at me through the slats in the blinds. Who the hell was that man? Why did he seem to hate me on sight? What strange power did he have over me that made me want desperately to see what he looked like under that thin shirt?

Four - The Alpha's Mark

"You sure you don't want me to stop at 24-Hour Urgent care? You might have banged your head harder than you think."

"I'm fine." Jake had just pulled off the Interstate again. We made a long, slow curve, and I could see the Woodland Motel just off the exit. It was a long, rectangular one-story motel that offered free HBO and 24-hour room service, or so it said from the tall flashing marquis high above it. "I really just want to get a shower and go to bed. I've got to deal with the rental car company and the body shop in the morning."

"So, where did you say you were headed again?"

I shrugged. "U. of M." I knew I should sound more excited when I said it. Tomorrow was supposed to be the first day of the rest of my life, and yet I felt lost and adrift.

"Go Blue," Jake said as he flicked his blinker on before making a right turn into the motel parking lot. "Here's hoping the new guy can get that football team turned around."

"Yeah," I said. "My Dad was a fan." The minute the words

Four - The Alpha's Mark

came out of my mouth, I wished I hadn't said them. I didn't want to answer questions about my personal life. Not with Jake. Not tonight.

"You a freshman?" Jake said as he pulled into a parking spot.

I nodded. Jake regarded me for a moment and then put the car in park and stepped around to get my door for me. It was sweet and chivalrous, and I felt like an ass for just wanting to finally have a few minutes to myself.

"You sure I can't call someone or do anything else for you?" Jake had the nicest puppy eyes, and it's possible he was trying to hit on me. I had terrible radar on that kind of thing.

The wind picked that moment to kick up again. The Woodland Motel was aptly named. Though it faced the highway, a Denny's, and three truck stops, the rear of the hotel butted up against a strip of dense woods. The tops of the tallest trees began to sway, and the temperature dropped quickly.

"I'm good," I said. "You've gone above and beyond the call of duty as it is. Have a good night."

"Oh, it was my pleasure. I'm just very thankful you didn't get hurt. It could have been a lot worse." Jake wasn't looking at me when he spoke. Instead, his eyes scanned the tree line. His fingers played at the handle of his holstered service weapon.

"Is something wrong?" I had to ask. Now that we were away from the specter of his boss, I had more than a passing curiosity about what had made him so angry back at the nature reserve outpost.

Jake shook his head but his eyes were still scanning the woods. "Nah," he finally said. "Just thinking we're in for a monster of a storm tonight. You'd better go ahead and get yourself checked in and stay indoors."

Four - The Alpha's Mark

"What was all of that back there?" I said, as I slung my backpack over my shoulder. "Was that your boss? Tuck? Is that what his name is?"

Jake's attention snapped back to me. "Tucker," he answered. "Yeah. He's kind of in charge, yes."

"Well, Mr. Tucker sure didn't seem like he was a very big fan of mine."

Jake fixed his smile back in place. "Don't pay that any mind. There's just a bunch of, uh, work stuff going on. Stressful day. Glad it's finally over."

His answer was less than convincing. His guarded posture didn't help. Well, whatever it was, I didn't see the need to borrow trouble. "Goodnight then," I said. "And thanks again for coming to my rescue. Please don't forget about the DNR."

Jake's mouth dropped then his eyes widened with understanding. "Right. Yeah. The wolf. That's already been taken care of. Don't you worry."

"Thanks." The memory of that poor, broken creature flashed through my mind again filling me with that strange sense of terrible loss. "Good night again."

Jake slapped his hand against the side of his leg and nodded one last time before he turned and got in his vehicle. He waited until I went inside the lobby door before shooting me a final wave, then pulling the cruiser out of the parking lot.

I turned and faced the desk clerk. "Had some excitement this evening?" The clerk was a middle-aged balding man with a sour, down turned mouth that didn't match the friendly gleam in his deep set eyes.

I smiled. "Fender bender. Do you have a non-smoking single?"

Four - The Alpha's Mark

He nodded. "Don't get a lot of activity here Tuesday nights. You can pretty much have your pick."

"How about the Presidential Suite?"

The clerk laughed and punched in an entry on his keyboard. "Good choice. Room 124. Second door when you walk out of the lobby. Check out's noon and the breakfast buffet will be set up here in the lobby by eight."

"Sounds like heaven." I slid my credit card across the desk. He gave me a key card in exchange. I gave the desk clerk a weak salute and headed out for Room 124.

The temperature had dropped probably another ten degrees by the time I walked outside again. The wind whipped through the trees, making them groan and howl loud enough to nearly drown out the freeway sounds. The hairs on the back of my neck rose as I had the sensation of being watched. Just like Jake had, I scanned the tree line, but saw nothing but pitch black and shaking foliage. I fumbled with the key card and went inside, grateful for the protection of four walls again.

I closed the door behind me and engaged the deadbolt. I grabbed the plastic rod hanging from the corner of the bay window next to the door and closed the heavy curtains. The room was small, square, and clean. I had one double bed, a T.V., and a table. The only thing I cared about in that moment was the presence of hot water. I crossed the room to the bathroom and turned on the bathtub knobs. Water blasted out of the faucet and turned hot almost instantly. I pulled up the metal plunger and switched the shower on. The water pressure was hard and steady. For the moment, this was my own little slice of heaven.

I peeled off my t-shirt and jeans. Under the harsh fluorescent lights, I finally got a look at the damage from the accident. I

Four - The Alpha's Mark

leaned across the sink and looked in the mirror. My bottom lip swelled a little where I'd struck it on the steering wheel. I fingered my jaw and moved it back and forth. It ached a little and I imagined I'd be sore in the morning. I had a little crust of blood just under my nose, but I was otherwise intact.

Lucky. So lucky. It could have been much worse, just like Jake said over and over. I peeled off my tank top and underwear, and kicked my clothes into a heap in the corner of the bathroom. I stepped under the shower and washed the day away. I hadn't packed any toiletries. My plan was to go shopping as soon as I got settled in the dorms. I'd just brought something to sleep in, and a change of clothes in my backpack. I wanted to start fresh. New clothes. New things. New life. I left most everything I owned in a storage unit back in Evanston. I'd sold the house and the money from that would get me comfortably through four years of college with what my scholarship didn't pick up. It was settled and arranged, and the right thing to do for all the wrong reasons. It felt like running away, except I had nothing to leave behind.

As the shower hit my skin, I threw my head back and let the water soak into my hair. I should have packed some product. The little motel shampoo and conditioner would be no match for my mass of hair. I had my mother's hair, dark, thick, and stick straight. I had her fair, freckled skin, and her pale green eyes. She died when I was seven, and watching me grow into the perfect copy of her both comforted and tortured my father.

"My beautiful Neve," he would say. "You've got the face of my Bonnie."

My heart ached at the loss of them both now. Nobody left but me. I was supposed to carry on for the two of them, when half the time all I wanted to do was curl into a ball and hibernate until the grief went away. It's what my father had done for a

Four - The Alpha's Mark

few years after ovarian cancer took Mom from us. And I was angry at him too. When he got his own diagnosis, I know a part of him saw it as a way to get back to her. Even though he had to leave me behind to do it.

I let out a hard breath as I fought to rinse the shampoo out of my tangled hair. I turned toward the water and let it hit my breasts. I swallowed a mouthful of water and tilted my head back. I did the one thing that drove the pain away. I took a deep breath and sang my go-to warm up piece.

"Ave Maria, gratia plena. Benedicta tu in mulieribus."

I hadn't done this in weeks. Months if I'm being honest. I sang this very song at my father's funeral mass surrounded by all the men of his station house. I still don't know how I got through it without breaking down. As I hit the sweeping high notes of Gounod's Ave Maria, a part of me hoped my father could still hear it. My voice was clear and strong, the acoustics of the bathroom perfect as they always are. I sang the chorus twice then opened my throat for the final line.

"In hora mortis nostrae Amen!"

I felt good. I felt clean. The power of my voice drove away the gloom and sadness that had hung over me since I'd encountered the wolf, and I felt strong again. It would be okay. I'd done what I could for her, and I'd done what I could for my father, too. They were at peace, even though I was still left behind.

I sluiced off the last of the soap, and turned off the water. Blinded in the steam, I reached for the stack of towels and tucked one around my body, and twisted the other around my hair. When I opened the door and stepped out of the bathroom, I heard it again. The slow, mournful wail of a creature in pain. I padded across the room and pulled back the corner

Four - The Alpha's Mark

of the curtain. I looked toward the woods, expecting to see those yellow eyes staring back at me. There was nothing, though.

I was just jumpy. That had to be it. I put on a fresh, white tank top and pink and green flannel shorts. My stomach roiled. In all the excitement I'd completely forgotten about dinner. I checked my phone. It was almost nine o'clock. I thought about the Denny's across the street, but didn't want to sit in a restaurant all alone. I peered through the curtain. The rain was coming, the trees whipped into a frenzy. At the end of the sidewalk in front of the motel, I saw the glowing lights of two vending machines.

"Carbs and sugar," I said. "Sounds perfect."

I grabbed the key card and five ones out of my backpack, slid into a pair of flip flops and headed down the sidewalk.

"Damn." I shivered as the air hit my skin. It had to have dropped to about forty degrees. "Pure Michigan, only here can it go from eighty to forty degrees in the space of four hours."

My vending machine choices were limited. I opted for a Diet Coke, cheese and crackers, a granola bar, and a bag of plain M&Ms. When the rain finally came, it fell hard and fast. If the sidewalk weren't under an awning, I would have gotten soaked again in a matter of seconds. The air was cool and clean. The scent of wet asphalt filled my nostrils as I turned back toward Room 124. I had that strange sensation of being watched again, and my focus went straight to the woods, but I saw nothing but the trees.

Three doors down from my room, I noticed a black Ford Pick-Up parked on a diagonal across the lot. I didn't remember it there when Jake dropped me off, and the way it was angled...it seemed pointed straight at Room 124.

Four - The Alpha's Mark

When my eyes met the driver's, I froze. Though I'd just met him, I'd know those eyes anywhere. Even across the parking lot I knew that flash of flint and silver. I don't know what made me do it. The wisest course would have been to go back to my room and lock the door behind me. But something drew me to him like a tractor beam.

I set the pop and candy on the sidewalk, and ran across the parking lot toward the truck. I forgot about the rain, I forgot about the cold. I was soaked to the bone with my hair plastered against my skin by the time I got there. I pounded on the driver's window with my palm.

"What are you doing?" he asked. He stared at me with those cruel, beautiful eyes. It was the same question I had for him.

"What do you want from me?" I said, wrapping my arms across my chest. I was fully drenched now and wearing nothing but my white tank top. He would be able to see my peaked nipples plainly if I moved my hands.

"Go back inside," he said, as if *I* were the one intruding on his personal space.

"Mr. Tucker," I said. "Is that your name? What the hell is going on?"

"Just Tucker," he answered. He was cool and casual while I felt like the Earth had shifted beneath my feet.

I meant to stomp my foot in indignation, to make him give me a straight answer as to why he seemed so pissed at me back at the cabin, and why the hell was he here now. But he was no longer looking at me. There was movement through the trees and when I followed his line of sight, I saw three pairs of menacing golden eyes weaving low and drawing closer.

"Shit," Tucker said. I stepped back as he climbed down from

the truck and slammed the door behind him. "Walk fast, don't run," he cautioned in a tone not much more than a growl. He gripped my upper arm and started to pull me with him. My flesh burned hot under his touch and I had to almost run to keep up with his long, powerful strides. He was so big. He towered over my 5' 3" height by more than a foot.

We got to the door of my room just as three wolves emerged from the tree line. Just as I'd known it when I saw Tucker's truck, I knew these wolves were here for me.

For all the latest on my new releases and a FREE COPY of the Sweet Submission EBOOK sign up for my newsletter. I promise, it's a spam free zone. You can unsubscribe anytime you like (I'll only cry a little). You can sign up here! http://www.kimberwhite.com/wild-lake-wolves/wild-lake-wolves-news

See you on the wild side!

Kimber

KimberWhite.com

kimberwhiteauthor@gmail.com

Books by Kimber White

Claimed by the Pack Series

The Alpha's Mark

Sweet Submission

Rising Heat

Pack Wars

Choosing an Alpha

The Complete Series Box Set

Wild Lake Wolves Series

Rogue Alpha

(featuring Mal from the Claimed by the Pack Series)

Dark Wolf (featuring Luke)

Primal Heat (featuring Bas)

Savage Moon (featuring Alec)

Hunter's Heart (featuring Derek)

Wild Hearts (Prequel featuring Pat Bonner)

Wild Ridge Bears Series

Lord of the Bears

Outlaw of the Bears

<u>Rebel of the Bears</u>

Curse of the Bears

Last of the Bears

<u>Mammoth Forest Wolves Series</u>

Printed in Great Britain
by Amazon